CLASS FAVORITE

Taylor Morris

ALADDIN MIX

NEW YORK   LONDON   TORONTO   SYDNEY

ALADDIN MIX

An imprint of Simon & Schuster Children's Publishing Division

1230 Avenue of the Americas, New York, NY 10020

Text copyright © 2007 by Taylor Morris

All rights reserved, including the right of reproduction in whole or in part in any form.

ALADDIN PAPERBACKS and related logo are registered trademarks of Simon & Schuster, Inc.

ALADDIN MIX is a registered trademark of Simon & Schuster, Inc.

Designed by Karin Paprocki

The text of this book was set in Bembo.

Manufactured in the United States of America

First Aladdin Paperbacks edition November 2007

10 9 8 7 6 5 4

Library of Congress Control Number 2007932711

ISBN-13: 978-1-4169-3598-8

ISBN-10: 1-4169-3598-3

0110 OFF

Acknowledgments

Thanks a million to everyone in mediabistro.com's novel workshop who gave me innumerable ideas and helped with every step along the way, even after the class ended. Thanks also to my West Coast reader, Jordana Brown, and my awesome agent, Steven Chudney. Thanks to my super editor, Molly McGuire, who always nudges me in the right direction. Special thanks to Sarah Rutledge, my amazing writing partner who has since become one of my best and dearest friends. And finally, to Silas, who always encourages me to try harder and dig a little deeper.

Does Your Crush Know You Exist?

You're walking—okay, drooling—along behind your crush when he unknowingly drops a pen from his backpack. You hurry to pick it up; when you give it to him, he says:

a) nothing, just accepts the pen and keeps walking.

b) "Thanks," and smiles at you before moving on.

c) "Thanks. How'd you do on that geometry quiz last week?"

The message of mass destruction arrived three days after I supposedly became a woman. It was Friday, February 14, to be exact. Happy Valentine's Day.

The day started off bad enough. I woke up with lingering cramps that no amount of Aleve could ease. I huddled in bed until I was almost late for school—I didn't have time to shower, even though my hair looked a little greasy. I put just a touch of baby powder on the shiniest parts, a tricky trick I learned in *Up!* magazine.

The Bowie Junior High office followed standard operating procedure by sending me a note during first-period English. It was a major coup to get one of these notes on Valentine's Day, since it was effectively rubbing your present in the faces of girls who were unloved by any boys. The office would receive the gift, and you could check it out between classes, but you couldn't pick it up until the final bell.

The student office assistant quietly handed the note to Ms. Galarza, whose eyes were gleaming with teacherly excitement. We were just beginning Jack London's *The Call of the Wild*, which some kids complained they'd already read in, like, fourth grade, but Ms. Galarza reasoned that we may have not fully understood it the first time. Up until that day, my thirteen-year-old life was more like The Call of the Mild, and there was no misunderstanding that fact.

I eagerly unfolded the note, which read simply, "You have a delivery in the office. You may come by after first period."

To get my attention, Arlene craned her neck over the row that separated us. Her winter-pale skin was already turning a warm brown now that softball season had started. I had tried to be an athlete with her, trying out for every sport from basketball to track—including, of course, softball. I not only never made the team, but something horrific usually happened during the tryouts. During volleyball tryouts last year, for example, I found it absolutely impossible to serve overhand—to the point that Coach Swathmore actually stopped the entire tryouts to ask, in front of everyone, "Kid, are you joking?" After claiming I wanted to concentrate on my B-average grades rather than sports, I gave up trying for good, and now watched from the sidelines as Arlene became better and better, and made more friends with each passing game.

Danielle Martin, who sat in the row between us, handed me a note from Arlene.

What is it?

A package?

After answering, I handed the paper to Danielle low and quick across the aisle.

From who?

Doesn't say.

"What do you think, Sara?" Ms. Galarza asked. Arlene and I quickly turned to the front as others turned to stare at us. Even Jason Andersen glanced back at me—just a glimpse, though, like he thought he heard something but only mildly cared to investigate.

"Uh," I began, trying to think of the most generic answer that would cover whatever she was asking. "I think so." I nodded, like *Yes, absolutely so.*

Ms. Galarza eyed me for a moment before saying, "I agree

with you. The dynamic between Buck and Spitz could easily be related to human interaction."

Letting out a quiet sigh of relief, I let my attention turn back to Jason. I gazed at the back of his head longingly. I'd known him since elementary, but he turned superhot this year—at least to me. He'd held reign as a nice, quiet guy since elementary school, neither nerdy nor great, although always very sweet, like the time he totally paid for Leslie Lasa's entire lunch even though she was only ten cents short. But something had changed in him over the summer. He seemed different now, like he sat up a little straighter, had a bit more confidence. Like he was more mature or something.

"I also want everyone to consider the relationship between man and dog," Ms. Galarza rambled. As if I could concentrate on anything, with Jason in front of me and that note in my hand.

Adults can be so dense—they wouldn't let me go see what was waiting in the office because they didn't want me to miss class. But they gave me this tease of a note, torturing me into sitting for another twenty-seven minutes wondering who, what, *why*? Had a secret admirer sent me a huge white teddy bear and a box of Russell Stover chocolates? Maybe it was that scrawny guy in my health class. I mean, I thought he just had a lazy eye, but maybe he'd really been gawking at me all this time. More likely, Dad had sent me something age-inappropriate from the road, like a Dora the Explorer sand bucket from Georgia. My dad took over his father's office-speaker business a couple of years ago and now travels around the southern states and North Texas installing these things that offices need for their intercom systems. He moved out in December when he and Mom officially separated, and even though he was always traveling for work and was rarely home, having him totally out of the house was weird. I still see him when he's in town, and we occasionally talk on the phone. But I missed the way he ruffled my hair in the morning when I was too cranky to talk, and the Saturday mornings he picked up doughnuts for us, always getting two of my favorite—Boston cream—in case someone got to it before I did. Even though he seemed to have forgotten that I am now a teenager and don't get as excited about Build-A-Bear as I used to, I still missed him more than I wanted to admit.

When the bell rang, Arlene bulldozed over people to get to my desk.

"Do you think it's flowers?" she shrieked, her blue eyes staring down at the pink office slip.

"I don't know," I said. I watched over her shoulder as beautiful, gorgeous, lovely Jason left. "I have no idea who would have sent them."

"Well, come on. Let's find out." Arlene pushed her way through the crowded halls, dragging me through the herd of students like a little sister being marched to Mom for punishment. " 'Scuse us," she said, pulling at my wrist as we came to the main hall, filled with trophy display cases and the 1989 Ball that won us our one and only state basketball championship. "Sorry, excuse me. Hi, Lindsay. Watch it, Shiner! Jerk! Excuse us, please. Oh, hey, Gerald."

I could smell the roses before we had even rounded the corner to the office. The front office literally looked like a florist's shop—it was absolutely stuffed with red and pink roses, and one lone bouquet of white roses with red tips.

"Oh, my God, look at all these." Arlene gasped.

"Dang. Think they're all from your mom's shop?" I asked as we pushed through the glass door.

"They sure don't look like they're from Kroger's," she said.

I quickly scanned the office, trying to pick out which bouquet might be mine. I tried real hard not to let myself think for even a second that they might be from some guy besides my dad—tried, but failed. I had a quick, unbelievable thought that this was Jason's way of telling me he's loved me since that day in third-grade recess when I accidentally stepped on his fingers on the jungle gym. After that, I knew I was only in for disappointment. What could top declaration-of-love flowers from Jason Andersen?

As Arlene scrambled around me to get a whiff, Mrs. Nicholson looked around her monitor, her chin jiggling in rhythm to the chains on her half-moon eyeglasses.

"Yes, girls?"

"She got a note," Arlene said, jerking her thumb in my direction.

Mrs. Nicholson, totally unimpressed, pointed her pen to the white flowers with red tips behind us. "Take the card, leave the flowers. You can pick them up after school."

"Oh, my God, you're so lucky!" Arlene sighed. "Look at these! They're so pretty. Who do you think they're from? Quick, here's the card." She plucked the little white, blank envelope from the baby's breath and quickly reached inside for the card.

"Here, give it to me." I snatched it away from her.

"Who's it from?" Arlene panted. I turned away as I pulled out the tiny card, because I had this really strong feeling that whatever was written there was going to change my little world. I rarely spoke to guys—I was hardly a master of seduction—but now I was getting a dozen white roses with gorgeous red tips. How could that not be something big?

When I turned my back to Arlene, I noticed someone sitting in the chair by the door, just across from my roses. She had ink-black hair set in a high ponytail, like a geyser of oil bursting out of the rubber band; she sat up straight, her hands gripping the sides of her chair and her crossed leg swinging nervously. I didn't know every kid at school, but I at least recognized them all; we rarely get any new kids in Ladel, and not in the middle of the school year, especially on a Friday, so I automatically wondered what her story was.

"Well?" Arlene shook my arm. She looked like she was about to bounce out of her well-worn Reeboks. "What does it say?"

The girl looked at me, and a soft smile spread across her shiny peach-colored lips. "Doesn't it feel good to be noticed?"

Arlene gave her a little, "Uh," her mouth dropping open. Arlene packs a lot into her one-syllable responses, and I knew this one meant, *Do you mind? We're in the middle of something important and totally private.* Besides, I wasn't so sure I agreed with the girl. I definitely hadn't wanted to be noticed that day last week when I slipped down the stairs on my way to class, landing so hard on my tailbone, I was afraid I'd broken it. I had wanted to rub my bum, but I bounced right back up, scooped up my books, and hollered to no one in particular, "See y'all next fall!"

I looked back at the card. As I read the few words, I felt the blood rush to my cheeks—and not in that girly, excited sort of way.

"So?" Arlene begged. "Who's it from?"

I shoved the card into the front pocket of my jeans, my hands already sweating as my mind raced on how to make this go away and wondering why, *why,* was this happening to me. Right then it absolutely did *not* feel good to be noticed. Nu-uh. Not at all.

"Nobody," I stumbled, "just . . . somebody." I glanced up at Mrs. Nicholson, and I swore she was looking at me funny—a bit of a smirk on her face. God, I thought. The envelope hadn't been sealed. She read it . . . *she knows.*

"What does that mean?" Arlene demanded as she followed me out of the office.

"Did you have to be rude to that girl?" I asked, wondering if I could transfer schools this late in the year.

"That's such crap, Sara. Why won't you tell me? I swear I won't tell *anyone*."

"Right," I said, twisting the combination on my locker. "Kind of like how you swore you wouldn't tell my sister what happened during basketball tryouts?" I had tried to go big by chucking the ball from the three-point line. I ended up decking Coach Swathmore in the face, breaking her nose. I was asked to leave the gym as quickly as her blood spilled to the court.

"Please! It was *funny*, and she would have found out, anyway. Elisabeth knows all the coaches here, and you said she talks to Coach Eckels, like, weekly. I saw her stop by just last week."

It was true. Coach Eckels had coached Elisabeth in cross-country when she was here at Bowie—he was the junior high's head coach and took a big interest in running. Since Elisabeth was such a star, he had given her extra coaching when she was here two years ago.

"Like I wanted everyone to know about that, much less *her*," I continued, trying to push the horror of the tiny card out of my mind. "Besides, I don't have to tell you everything, you know."

Lately, I'd been getting agitated with Arlene. We've been

best friends since elementary school, but even though I still considered her *my* best friend, sometimes I wondered if I was still *her* best friend. To keep us connected after she started playing softball, we started a Golden Raspberry–movie tradition because we both secretly love movies that get horrible reviews, so we decided to embrace them. The Razzies are like the anti-Oscars—they're awards that movies and actors get for being the absolute worst. We watch them the first Saturday night of every month, except for that time in October that Arlene's softball team had some big team-bonding sleepover. I was mad about it, but I never told her. I didn't want to seem like a crybaby, but she had sacrificed *our* friendship bonding for her teammates. That stung.

I slapped my locker shut and started down the hall, trying to act normal when really I was dying of anger and embarrassment.

"You know, I could just ask my mom who sent them. I'm sure they came from her shop," Arlene called out in a half-hearted threat.

"Yeah," I said, trying to sound casual as I rounded the corner. "But you won't."

I really, truly, sincerely hoped I was right.

I always thought that getting my period would herald my arrival as a woman. Along with the inconvenience of that monthly visitor, I'd also be rewarded with the perks:

My boobs and hips would suddenly fill out, my hair would be shinier, my voice would have a coquettish lilt, and all the guys would want me.

I was patient for this day to arrive—at first. When Becca Miller got her period in fifth grade, some girls teased her about it even though we were completely curious about what it felt like. In sixth grade I looked enviously at girls wearing kitten heels and showing off new belly button piercings— signs of womanhood, in my mind, not to mention things my mother would never let me wear. When Arlene discreetly got her period that year, I felt betrayed. Until then, we had done everything together—shaving our legs for the first time and flirting with boys at the same party (different guys!). I found out three months later, when she casually said, "I have *the worst* cramps." When I asked why she hadn't told me, she said, "Gross, Sara. It's not the kind of thing you discuss," even though she just had.

Suddenly we were entering junior high, where the girls wore makeup, shorter skirts, and kissed boys. Then there was me. I wasn't allowed to wear makeup yet, my legs were too scrawny to wear short skirts, I'd never had a boyfriend, *plus* I hadn't gotten my period yet. I felt like a fraud. It was not the image I had of starting junior high. Then, in October of our seventh-grade year, everyone had a date to the Fall Ball—including Arlene, even though we had sworn we'd turn up our noses at the event to stay home and watch Razzies. When some random guy from the baseball team asked her to go, she acted all giddy about it, and the next thing I knew, I was sitting home alone watching *From Justin to Kelly* with no one to make sarcastic comments to.

It wasn't until this year, in eighth grade, that I finally got my period. Call it an early Valentine's gift. There was no joy in the big moment, only a feeling of *God, it's about freaking time.* I realized I looked no different from the day before, but I did feel different—as in yuckier.

"I can't believe you still won't tell me. What's the big secret?"

Arlene started in on me when we met outside the cafeteria. All the girls were talking excitedly about who had gotten flowers, who had sent them, and the bigger scandal of who *hadn't* received any. (Word was that Kayla Cane, who normally made sure she had a boyfriend around Valentine's Day, hadn't received any.) I had come up with a brilliant plan to handle the situation: I would ignore it and hope that it went away.

At the front of the lunch line, I pulled a five-dollar bill from my front pocket and felt the soft bits of the now-torn card. I had peeked at it in second period, just to make sure I had read it correctly.

**YOU'VE FINALLY ENTERED WOMANHOOD,
AND I COULDN'T BE PROUDER.
CONGRATULATIONS . . . PERIOD!
LOVE, MOM**

It was written in another woman's handwriting—Arlene's mom? She owned It's About Bloomin' Time, the one florist in Ladel, Texas. It proved that someone else, other than myself and my mother, knew about the flowers and my period.

This was all my sister's fault—she was the one who had told on me. Just as we were running out the door that morning, late already, Elisabeth had said, right in front of Mom, "Sara, did you tell Mom you finally got your period?"

"Elisabeth!"

"What? God, grow up already," she said, like it was no big deal after all.

Mom had inhaled a little gasp and flashed a proud smile. "Sara, honey!" she said. "You finally got it!"

I grabbed a carton of nonfat milk at the front of the lunch line, took the change for my cheese enchilada lunch from Lunchlady Campbell, who, sorry, looks like a linebacker, and walked with Arlene to a table. Sometimes we sat by ourselves, and sometimes a few of her softball friends joined us. When they sat with us, all they talked about softball: the teams they were playing, who was hitting what average that season—in other words, boring stuff. When they tried to include me in the conversation, it was, "Are you going to try out next season?" They were just making conversation, but it stunk because, as I had thoroughly demonstrated at more than one tryout, I had zero athletic coordination.

Arlene and I sat down, alone for now, thank God, until . . .

"Sara! I just saw my roses in the office and saw your name on the white ones. Who sent them? They're awesome." Ellen Spitz had barely said a word to me until now. She plopped her beige lunch tray on our table and sat down across from me. She was the shortstop on Arlene's team, a member of FFA—the Future Farmers of America—and wore extra-heinous boots, jeans, and Garth Brooks–esque shirts. Every single day. That day, it was green Rocky Mountain jeans with purple Justin Ropers. I kid you not. And I thought my Old Navy clothes made me fashionably challenged.

I lifted my fork to my mouth, cheese and grease dripping from it, and delicately blew on the enchilada. My stomach was all cramped up—I couldn't tell if it was from period misery or the massive dread of my flower secret being revealed.

"She won't even tell *me*," Arlene assured Ellen. "What's the big deal?" she asked, turning on me. "Why won't you tell us?"

"Hey, Sara," said Shiner. He stood in the aisle next to our table, carrying two Cokes on his enchilada tray. He wore a Dallas Cowboys puffy jacket with shorts and a coral choker he got in Tampa three summers ago and hadn't taken off since. "Nice flowers, *mamacita*." He laughed his squawking laugh. *"Ha-ha-haaa!"*

I fumed at Shiner for getting a thrill out of my pain *and* for mentioning anything mother related. To think that I had actually worried that it was just a "Hi! Miss you and love you" gift from the road from my dad. I wondered if he'd call to wish me a happy Valentine's Day.

Shiner got his nickname from the sixth-grade baseball guys. He had taken a baseball to his left eye three times throughout the season, leaving him with a black eye for two months. Nobody called him Jimmy—his real name—except the teachers, and I didn't even like looking at him since that night at the Fall Ball earlier this year.

I flicked my wrist as dismissively as I could, even though I was cringing with embarrassment inside. "Just walk away."

Shiner snorted, and looked like he was about to say something, but he didn't.

It's strange how people end up. Shiner and I actually used to play together every now and then at recess when we were kids. Then, at this year's Fall Ball, everyone, including Arlene, who went stag with me slow-danced at the end of the night while I stood sheepishly in the corner, trying not to be noticed. To my surprise, Shiner came over and asked me to dance. We hadn't talked much since the days of recess had ended, and I was mostly glad that someone had asked me to dance. As we shuffled across the floor of the cafeteria, which served as our dance hall, Kayla Cane and her boyfriend of the night glided by us. Kayla looked me up and down, then looked at Shiner and threw her head back and laughed. I felt like an instant loser. When I looked at Shiner, whose jaw was clenched, I saw the pimples on his cheeks and the way his nostrils flared as he breathed. I felt how bony his shoulders were, and how sweaty his palms. Before the song even ended, I muttered a thanks and went back to my corner. We hardly made eye contact after that, and lately we've resorted to smart-aleck remarks.

"Lovely," I said, turning back to my grease and cheese as Shiner did, in fact, walk away. "He is such a loser."

"I saw him outside in the courtyard blowing his nose," Arlene said, "without a tissue. Just plugged one nostril and blew out the other."

"Disgusting." I cringed.

"I don't know," Ellen said. "He seems okay. I mean, he never did anything to me. Anyway, the flowers are gorgeous, Sara. You have to tell us who sent them." She stood and picked up her tray. "I'm sitting with the girls," she said to Arlene. "We heard that the Crawford pitcher is at least sixteen. See you at practice." And off she bounced.

"Did she have to take Shiner's side?" I asked. "He made fun of me first." Arlene stared over at the girls softball table and

I realized, with another punch in the gut, that she'd probably rather be with them than with me. "If you want to go sit with them, you can," I said, even though I didn't want her to.

"No, no," she said, shaking her head. She tucked her hay-colored hair behind her ear. "Don't worry about Shiner. Or Ellen. She was just saying."

"Whatever. Cramps make you moody, right?" I asked as I rubbed my hand across my stomach.

"God, yes. Still, if someone had sent me flowers, I don't know how I could let anything put me in a bad mood."

I sighed. Maybe I needed an ally in this. Maybe I'd feel better if I told Arlene, who was, after all, my official best friend. Maybe it was her duty to know things like this about me, even if we weren't as close as we used to be.

So I took a deep breath and said, "Okay, I'll tell you who sent them, but you have to swear on your softball glove that you won't tell anyone. Not a single soul."

Arlene's eyes widened with anticipation, and she nodded furiously. "I swear, I swear, I swear I will not tell another single living soul for as long as I live. Cross my heart."

So I told her. I trusted her. Because what had she ever done to betray me?

♥ 2 ♥

Are You the Keeper of Secrets
or the Disher of Gossip?

You've stepped out of your sociology class to go to the bathroom. On the way back, you hear Angie Slater whispering into her cell phone, "I can't believe Joann got suspended for plagiarism." You:

a) discreetly walk away, but decide to tell **only** your best friend, and **only** after making her swear not to tell another single living soul.

b) tell no one, since the news doesn't even affect you.

c) shuffle away quickly, heart racing with excitement; when you get back to class, you tell what's-her-name across the aisle what you just heard.

I KNOW SOMETHING ABOUT YOU.

The ripped and folded piece of spiral notebook paper had been slipped to me during Ms. Cowell's fifth-period science class by someone in the desk behind me. For weeks the seat had been empty, and today I'd come in late and hadn't noticed anyone there.

"Sara Thurman," Ms. Cowell had announced when I came in after the bell. "You're *late*." Like it's such a huge offense.

I'd been in the nurse's office trying to score some sweet pain meds for my cramps, but all I got was two generic aspirins with an added dose of questioning about the flowers from Nurse Windham, as well as a maintenance guy who was changing a lightbulb.

"Sorry," I mumbled as I slipped into my seat.

Ms. Cowell was yapping about motion. I wasn't really listening. For one, I thought it was too early in the second semester for her to say anything test-worthy. Also, I couldn't stop thinking about my mother and how I would deal with her when I got home. I couldn't believe that only last weekend I had thought my life was so dull.

I looked over my shoulder to see who had written the cryptic note, and all I could see was a mop of black hair. I guessed it was the girl who had been in the office earlier. She had held the folded paper out to me low, by my waist, with long, natural nails gripping the sides. When a note is offered, you accept it.

"What do you think, Jimmy?" Ms. Cowell asked Shiner. I snapped to attention, quickly folding the note back and clutching it under my desk.

"Ma'am?" Shiner's eyes were glassy with disinterest. When he leaned forward to search his textbook for an answer, the numbers from his Emmitt Smith jersey peeled off the back of the chair.

"Please, everyone." Ms. Cowell sighed. "Let's pay attention. If this notebook is sitting in the front seat of a car," she continued, her voice raised a little louder, waving her teacher's notebook at us, "and the car is traveling at sixty-five miles per hour, is the notebook moving? Jimmy? What do you think?"

Shiner tapped his black Bic pen on his desk, thoughtfully and unsurely. "I'd say . . . no?"

"No, the notebook is not moving?"

"Yeah. No."

I wondered where the new girl came from. I wondered why she'd had to move to a new school midyear and start on a Friday, no less. Mostly, though, I hoped her note wasn't about the flowers. I slumped down in my chair and watched Shiner squirm under questioning.

"The book is stationary," Ms. Cowell coaxed Shiner, "even if the car is traveling at sixty-five miles per hour, correct?"

"Yeah?" Shiner shrugged.

"Does everyone agree with this?" Ms. Cowell asked, looking to the rest of us.

I looked around the room. The six even rows of sandbox-brown desks with attached chairs held students slumped in various forms of boredom: Some leaned forward, chins rested in hands, while others sat back, their hands stuffed in their pockets. I sat with a stiff back, panicked with curiosity, clinging to the note in my now-sweaty palm.

"Although that does make some sense," Ms. Cowell continued, "the notebook *is* in motion, because it is being propelled by the car. The notebook, you, your backpack—everything that's in the car is in motion. This is called *relative motion*. And that *will* be on the test," she added.

Laboriously, in unison, we uncapped our pens, opened our notebooks, and wrote this term down. I underlined it and put stars on either side of it. **TEST!!** I wrote.

For the rest of the period, I tried to pay attention to Ms. Cowell, but it was impossible. Who was this girl, and what did she know?

Finally, the bell rang. Ms. Cowell, jolted out of her lecture euphoria, quickly hollered out, "Please write a two-page summary on motion. And don't forget your worksheets are due next Friday!"

I stacked my textbook on top of my spiral, dropped my pen in my bag, and nervously turned to the girl behind me.

"Hey," I said.

We stood facing each other, holding our books to our chests like shields. I was immediately transfixed by her eyes— they were bright green, like a traffic light, and lined in black.

She wore a tight sweater, the ends of the sleeves covering her hands.

"Sara?" she asked as she swung her big black leather bag over her shoulder.

"Yeah. You're the girl I saw in the office this morning, right?"

"Yep, that was me. I'm Kirstie Luegner," she said.

As we walked down the hall, I could feel other students' curious eyes on her. I'd gone to school with the same people since kindergarten—we rarely got new blood. One glance at Kirstie and you could instantly tell she wasn't from around here, and it wasn't just her high-heeled boots. It was something about the way she carried herself—she seemed a little more self-assured than the rest of us.

"Can you help me find my locker?" she asked. "All these halls look the same."

I knew exactly what she meant. Not that I ever gave much thought to architectural design, but I always thought a box-shaped building was aiming a little low.

"It took me a month of going into the wrong classrooms," I confessed. "Three times in one week I sat in an honors algebra class, wondering why I didn't understand anything the teacher said." Kirstie laughed, and I was encouraged. "I kept going back, because I was recognizing the people in there. When I finally realized what I was doing, I was all, 'Oh! I thought this was honors calculus!' Like our school even offers calculus."

"Don't feel bad," she said. "In the five hours I've been here I've gotten in trouble for chewing gum and I already know the gossip. I feel totally pathetic."

"Yeah, so . . . ," I began. "What gossip *do* you know?"

Kirstie looked at the bank of lockers we had arrived at and found hers. "Well, I feel weird telling you—I don't even know you. But I heard some girls talking after lunch," she said as she tossed in her science book and grabbed a history book. "First of all, remember that I'm just the messenger, okay?" She eyed me eagerly.

"Yeah, I know," I answered anxiously.

"Okay. These girls were laughing their butts off—at you. I couldn't hear all of the conversation, but they were saying something about period roses. Then one of them said how great it'd be to bring you a huge gift-wrapped box tomorrow . . . of the biggest, fattest, granniest Kotex ever. Practically diapers. So big, this girl said, that it wouldn't even fit in your locker and you'd have to carry it around all day. She said it'd be a great follow-up to the roses your mother sent. I can't believe your mom did that," Kirstie said as she slapped her locker shut. "That's rough."

"Wait," I asked. "You know about those roses?"

She looked at me guiltily and said, "I thought everyone knew."

My heart pounded and my breath quickened. "Well, what did they look like, the girls you saw?"

"There was a blond girl. Oh, and the other was a brunette."

"Great. You just described every girl in school."

"Sorry to deliver such awful news," Kirstie said sympathetically. "I feel horrible telling you. I know how terrible it is to be gossiped about. I just thought you'd want to know. I know I would." She looked down the thinning halls. "I'm gonna be late. I've got history with Mrs. Hanson. Is she a witch?"

"No. She's old. Look, are you sure . . ."

"Listen. Come over to my house tonight and we'll talk about it. You can spend the night and we'll do spa treatments. My mom just got this facial stuff from Sweden. It makes your skin feel like silk."

I felt like I had to reshift my mind. I was trying to process what she had just told me, and then she was asking me over to her house. I have to say that it was the first time someone other than Arlene had asked me to spend the night since I don't know when. It felt good, if a little odd. "Thanks," I said, "but I have plans." My plans involved yelling at my mom before having a total and complete meltdown in the privacy of my own bedroom.

"Then come over on Saturday," she said.

"Actually, I have plans with my best friend on Saturday."

"Then Sunday," she said. As she waited for me to answer, I felt like her eyes were challenging me. I wasn't sure what her deal was—just one hallway back I was thinking how self-assured she was, and now she was grilling me about coming over. I wasn't trying to blow her off, but I got the feeling she thought I was.

"The thing is," I began, "my best friend and I have this movie thing that we do. We start it Saturday night and it goes until the Academy Awards on Sunday." I smiled to show her that I was sincere, because I was. It was a big event for me and Arlene—I even got special permission to stay over at her place until the awards ended late on Sunday night.

"We have a huge TV and an amazing sound system at my house. You could both come over and watch. We could even dress up like the stars. I'll order Italian—I'll pay."

The thought of watching the Academy Awards with some-one other than Arlene would be like having a family portrait taken with your neighbor.

I guess I hesitated too long, trying to think up a nice way of explaining it to her, because she quickly said, "Oh, forget it. I don't mean to be pushy. I was just trying to be nice. Because, no offense, but you look like you just lost your best friend."

I didn't know what to think, except that she had to be mistaken about what she had heard. For three years I'd been a nobody at this school. No one teased me and no one sang my praises (of which I had none). Suddenly I wished I were as invisible as I had been yesterday.

"Don't look so worried," Kirstie said, walking toward the stairwell as I stood immobile. "It's going to be fine, I promise," she called, the last word echoing off the stairwell.

I didn't have much time to think about what Kirstie had told me.

When I got to Mrs. Everly's algebra class, I noticed a tampon wrapper beneath my desk. I stood frozen in the aisle, staring down at it. I tried to tell myself that it was only an unfortunate coincidence while trying to look normal and unfazed.

As everyone settled down and the bell rang, Sean Hurley, who could be cool when he wanted to but apparently never felt the need, coughed. He got a good laugh out of the people around him, so he did it again.

"On the rag!" he hacked into his balled fist.

Richie Adams, a killer athlete and friend of Jason's, laughed so hard, he doubled over.

"Dude," he gasped to Sean as he tried to control himself.

I sat up straighter as if they had nothing to do with me, then I covered the wrapper with my shoe as if it weren't even there. Everything was fine, I told myself. Just another day in algebra. It'd all be over soon, and then I could go home, slaughter my mother, and transfer schools. Then Shiner walked in.

"Hello, Sara. Period," he began in an oh-so-normal-but-not-really voice. "How're you doing? Period. Have a good day. Period."

What an idiot. He couldn't even get a mean joke right. A sick feeling came to my stomach as Shiner sat in his seat, and I could feel my heart pumping. Kayla Cane, whose skin was turning a weird orange the warmer the weather got, was giggling at something Richie said; when she caught me looking, her kohl-lined eyes glared back at me. Sean Hurley said from across the room, "Hey, Thurman. Need a quarter for the girls' room machine?" And then he flicked one at me.

It landed by my feet, and I stared down at it. My face burned hot red—a color I now absolutely hated. Everyone in class roared with laughter, which of course Mrs. Everly didn't notice because the woman is so deaf, she needs a hearing aid to hear herself talk. Rosemary Vickers, last year's Class Favorite, swatted Sean and told him to shut up, and I loved her for it. Right then I vowed that if she were nominated again this year, I'd totally vote for her.

Keeping my foot covered over the tampon wrapper, I leaned over and retrieved the quarter. "Thanks," I said. "I was one short for the Coke machine." I shoved it in my pocket and sat back in my seat.

When class started, I braved a look at Jason—he was looking right at me. He smiled a little smile and rolled his eyes. I rolled my eyes back, feigning indifference, but I could feel my chin quivering, a huge sob trying to bust through. Maybe he felt my pain, having gone through some major, school-wide embarrassment himself earlier this year at football tryouts. I heard from Arlene, who kept up with such things, that he had lobbed a football toward a wide receiver, slamming the ball into the water table, and later got the wind knocked out of him by Keith Robinson, who is so scrawny, he makes Shiner look like the Hulk. Like my attempt at basketball tryouts, Jason didn't make the football team, but he's on the basketball team, and Arlene says he's pretty good. I took comfort in the fact that I had a fellow menace-in-arms when it comes to sports, at least a little bit.

All through class, I was tormented by thoughts of how word had already escaped about why I got those roses. I'd told Arlene, but I knew that there was no way she would break my confidence. Sure, she had told my sister about my basketball tryout debacle, but that was different. I guess in a couple of years I'd agree with her that it had been funny. Arlene had a big mouth, but she'd never betray me like this. I just didn't get it.

Thank God it's Friday, I thought. The weekend meant Saturday night and all of Sunday with Arlene, checking out the Razzie winners online as well as the Academy Awards on Sunday. Things would get better quickly.

Then I remembered I still had to go home and face my mother.

Can You Turn Your Sibling Spats into Something Special?

True or False: When it comes to sharing clothes, your sister knows that what's yours is hers, and vice versa.

"You're *late*."

That was the first thing Elisabeth said when I emerged from the sanctity of my room, where I'd hunkered down since coming home from school. She was already sitting at her place at the table, her wavy chestnut hair falling gracefully down her back.

I looked at my dad's empty chair and felt the enormity of my day. "You're ugly," is what I said back to her as I took a seat.

"Just because you have no plans tonight doesn't mean the rest of us are losers who have all the time in the world," she said. I knew Elisabeth had a date later that night. By the time she was my age, she's already had three boyfriends.

"Don't call me a loser, loser," I said back.

"Girls," my mother said in a vaguely warning tone as she brought a pitcher of iced tea to the supper table. "Be nice, now. It's Valentine's Day." She sat down, then cut a slice of meat loaf and held it out to me, waiting for me to bring my plate closer.

"I'm not hungry," I grumbled. Mom held the meat loaf in midair, as if expecting me to change my mind. I responded with, *"Mother."*

"I'll take that, Mom," Elisabeth offered, matching my mother's horrific trill of happiness. "I'm *starving*."

"Elisabeth, sugar, you're most certainly *not* starving," Mom said. This was one of her pet peeves. "Children in Africa are starving—dying of hunger, bodies wasted, stomachs bloated. You're just hungry, I'm sure."

I gave Elisabeth a *ha-ha* grin.

"So, Sara," Mom began, smiling as she sipped her iced tea. "Did anything interesting happen today?"

"Yeah, actually, something did."

"Excuse me?" Mom held her glass above the table, frozen, just as she was about to set it down.

"Yes, ma'am," I corrected. "Something *did* happen. I was completely humiliated in front of the entire school because of you." My heart was pumping in my chest, and I knew I'd get in trouble if I spoke to her too loudly or sharply. "Mom, I can't believe you would do that. Why did you do that?"

I wasn't looking at Elisabeth, but I could feel her grow still with interest. She was going to love making fun of me for this one.

"What are you talking about, *at school*?" Mom asked.

"The *flowers*?" I said, unable to believe she was even asking.

"Hey, why'd she get flowers?" Elisabeth chimed in, her voice thick with jealousy.

"Your sister is now a woman." Mom actually said this with a straight face.

"Mom! Come on!" I wailed.

"What's this about school?" Mom asked again. "I had Arlene's mom deliver them here so they'd be waiting for you when you got home."

"Well, guess what? She sent them to school, and everybody found out about them. You're so embarrassing!" I yelled, a cry forming way in the back in my throat.

"You sent her flowers for her *period*?" Elisabeth's eyes squinted as she tried to comprehend the unreality of it.

"Slow down, Sara," Mom said, ignoring Elisabeth. "There must have been a mistake. I *think* I told her to send them here. . . ."

"Oh, wow . . . ," Elisabeth muttered from across the table, the hungry smile gone from her face.

"That's just great," I said. "It doesn't matter now, Mother, because everyone at school found out who sent them and why. I might as well die and move to Waco."

"Look, honey. I'm sorry about the mix-up, but this *is* a big event in your life. And if you need any help learning how to—"

"Mother! I can't believe you! You're so humiliating!"

"Watch your mouth, young lady," she said, pointing her fork at me.

"You're such an embarrassment," I continued. "Everyone in my class was making fun of me. Do you know what that's like?"

"Oh, honey." Mom sighed. "I really am sorry. I meant to have them sent here."

"Well, it's too late," I said, folding my arms across my stomach. I knew Mom was being sincere, but her nice gesture was turning into one whopper of a problem for me. "Nobody in the entire school even knew who I was before this. Now *everyone* knows who I am." My vision became blurry from the wetness in my eyes as I picked up my napkin to wipe at them. "Just because you and Dad split up doesn't mean I need you to obsess over me."

"Sara, I was just trying to do something nice."

"You're only making everything worse."

"That's enough," she snapped. "Now, I'm sorry the flowers were sent to school instead of here, but I had the best of intentions, and you know it. The least you can say is thank you. Just go on to your room. I've had about enough of this."

"Fine! I don't care," I yelled as I threw my napkin on the table.

"Sara! One more word out of you . . ."

I stomped down the hall and slammed the door to my room.

I lay on my bed, my face mushed in my pillow, sticky from crying. The day had been more than I could handle.

I sat up, rubbed my swollen eyes, and took a deep breath.

I picked up my so-outdated see-through phone and began dialing Arlene's number. I had totally lost it at dinner, but I told myself I was allowed the freak-out, considering. Now, though, I had to pull myself together and figure out how to fix this. I had to make sure Arlene hadn't told anyone about the flowers, and ask her if she knew of any gift-bearing pranks against me. It couldn't wait until our Razzie/Academy Awards party on Saturday.

When Arlene answered her cell, I could hear girls laughing in the background, and a distant horn honking.

"Is this a bad time?"

"What? Oh, yeah, it's fine. Knock it off!" Arlene called, her laugh coming through muffled on the phone, as if she were covering up the mouthpiece. Someone squealed, and there was more laughing.

"Forget it," I said, not wanting to talk about the flowers with the other girls listening. "I'll talk to you later."

"We just finished practice," she continued. "I'm with Megan, Rachel, and Ellen. Rachel's sister Betsy is taking us to get something to eat."

I felt that, with each passing softball game, Arlene racked up more new friends. "Really, I can just talk to you tomorrow."

"That's a red light!" Arlene called. "Oh, my God," she said to me. "Betsy totally almost went through a red light. You're going to get us all killed!"

"Look, I have to ask you a really important question."

"Yeah, what is it?"

"You didn't tell anyone what I told you earlier, did you?"

"Tell anyone what?"

"You know, *what I told you*," I emphasized.

"What, about your mom?"

"God, Arlene! Not in front of those girls."

"Oh, they don't know what I'm talking about." I heard one of the girls call, "What *are* you talking about?" Arlene hollered, "Nothing," and they all started laughing again.

"You're sure? Because word got out, and you're the only one I told." I knew there was an accusatory tone in my voice, but I was getting anxious, and she wasn't listening.

"By the way," she began. "I had to head off a major rumor for you today."

"Perfect," I grumbled. "I don't need rumors. I already have gossip."

"Ellen heard from someone that Shiner sent you those roses. Can you imagine? I knew you'd just die if anyone thought that for a moment, so I totally cleared it up."

"Cleared it up? What does that mean?"

"She thought *Shiner* sent you the roses," she repeated. The voices in the car were getting louder as the girls sang along to the radio.

"I heard you, Arlene. Who did you tell *what*?"

"Look, I can barely hear you, Sar. I'm sorry—I'll call you later, 'kay? Hello?"

I sat silently. I didn't expect Arlene to drop everything for me, but I wanted her to tell me that *heck no* she didn't tell anyone about the roses, and that she was sorry that Valentine's Day had turned out so rotten for me. To be honest, hearing her carefree laughter with a bunch of girls who weren't my friends made me jealous—jealous at her for having a fun day, jealous because she had more friends than me, and jealous that she had something to do on a Friday night that didn't involve me. I started to wonder about friendship, and how friends were supposed to comfort each other, be there for each other. I didn't feel like Arlene was doing that at all. She wasn't even thinking about how I felt. And the frightening truth was, she was the only person who knew why I got those roses. I rubbed my swollen eyes, holding back tears.

"Sara, you still there? I think I lost her," she said to her friends, and then she hung up the phone.

Are you open to new friendships?

A new girl arrives in your civics class and asks you if she can sit with you at lunch. You:

a) ask her what type of clique she hung out in at her last school so you can fairly decide if she's a fit for your clique.

b) tell her of course she can sit with you, and you'll meet her at her locker and escort her to the cafeteria just to make sure she doesn't get lost.

c) tell her, "*No habla English.*" Why is that stranger talking to you?!

Like I said, Arlene and I have this ritual of watching Golden Raspberry movies every month where we get together, eat junk food, and watch the worst-of-the-worst movies, like *Battlefield Earth* and *Gigli*. We love cringing at the bad acting, dialogue, and general heinousness of these movies. They are the type of movies that no one except your best friend would watch with you, and we both love it.

The Razzie "winners" of the year are announced the night before the Academy Awards. I always go to Arlene's house and we look up the winners online and immediately put the best of the worst at the top of our must-see list. The best/saddest is when one actor or actress is dishonored year after year. For example, Haden Prescott is a repeat offender—she's been dishonored three times in four years. At the rate she was going, reality game shows couldn't be far behind. But this year, something phenomenal happened. Haden Prescott was nominated for a Razzie *and* an Academy Award in the same year. It was unprecedented.

When I arrived at Arlene's on Saturday night, I felt uneasy about what Kirstie had told me, and even worse about calling Arlene to question her on how word got out about the roses. But when she told me the pizza was on its way, her computer was rolling (the ceremony only showed online), and her family was under explicit instructions not to bother us, I told myself not to worry or even think about what had happened at school yesterday. The worst was already over, and the rest would turn out to be nothing.

"What happened yesterday?" Arlene asked as soon as we were in her room. "We were talking and the next thing I knew, you were gone."

"Oh," I said. "I think your phone cut me off." I hated lying to her, but I didn't want to relive the whole thing either. I wished I could travel back in time, like in Haden Prescott's movie *Not Again!* where she keeps living the same day over and over again (like *Groundhog Day*, but not funny). I would go to It's About Bloomin' Time and make sure the flowers were to be sent home and not to school. Then my life would be its usual, boring self.

"Did you hear me tell you that Ellen heard a rumor that Shiner sent you those flowers?"

"Yeah, I heard. Hey, you want to make bets on if Haden wins the Razzie? I'll give you odds," I said, even though I had no idea what that meant—I'd just heard it from movies.

"With a title like *Demon's Lover*, I'd say she's got a pretty good chance." In the comedy, Haden played the spawn of Satan who falls in love with a pastry chef and tries to save mankind.

"I know! We have to rent it immediately," I said, happy that I had so easily turned the conversation away from the flowers.

"We'll get it before our next party, for sure," Arlene said.

As we settled in for the evening—Arlene picked off half her pepperonis and I ate them, just like we always did—I almost did forget about the flowers and the fact that somehow word had gotten out. Even though she was the only person who knew why I got them, I told myself that if she had slipped and told someone, she would have told me. I shouldn't doubt her. I shouldn't even question her—that would be borderline insulting, like I was questioning her friendship. Sure, she hadn't always been the greatest at keeping secrets, but with a juicy one this big, she wouldn't betray me.

When Haden Prescott won the worst actress Razzie, Arlene said, "Next stop, reality TV!"

I fell asleep that night thinking about Haden and wondering if she would win the Academy Award. She was a long shot— the other actresses she was up against had all been nominated before. But maybe, I thought, drifting off, maybe she would surprise us all.

The next day we about burned our eyes out watching all the preshow stuff. E! did a whole thing on the nominees, where they had started, the TV shows they'd done, the movies they'd made. Although they mentioned Haden's Razzie-nominated movies, they never once said the words *Golden Raspberry Award*.

"How could they not mention that?" I asked.

Arlene popped a cherry sour ball in her mouth and said, "'Cause. *These* awards are about respect. They wouldn't give the Razzies the satisfaction of mentioning them in the same breath as the Academy Awards."

As pictures of Haden flashed on the screen, the voice-over said, *"She's struggled in Hollywood for years for the chance to be taken seriously as an actress, but with bit roles and questionable movies, her journey has been an uphill battle. But Haden has endured and, with* The Silent Widow, *has proven herself as worthy an actress as the other women in her category."*

The entertainment-news guy said to the camera: "Yes, we're certainly rooting for her to win, but the truth is, Haden Prescott is already a winner, just by being nominated. She's already landed roles in films from such directors as Nicolas Capicaccio and Stephen Allman. It seems that, as an actress, Ms. Prescott has finally come into her own."

When the awards finally began, I rooted for Haden. She looked beautiful in her golden sequined gown, all poised and elegant. Nothing of the Satan-spawned hottie remained in the woman who sat in the plush red velvet seats of the Kodak Theatre in Hollywood.

"I can't believe she went from the D-list to an Academy Award nominee just like that." I snapped my fingers for emphasis.

"I know," Arlene said. "It just goes to show that any loser can turn it around. She went from reject to royalty in just a couple of months."

Even though Haden didn't win, I still felt that what Arlene said was true: Anyone can turn it around. Just like that. Maybe even me.

As I walked through Bowie's front doors on Monday morning, I felt sick to my stomach, and it wasn't because of cramps, which had mostly passed, thank goodness. I hoped with all hope that everyone would have forgotten about the flowers. I wasn't sure that I had the energy to keep dodging comments about who sent them or if I needed more feminine products. I tried to remember how I'd felt hanging out with Arlene all weekend—how tight our friendship was, and how what Kirstie heard didn't make sense.

Before first period, Kirstie appeared next to my locker as I spun the combination. "Why didn't you call me back?"

I put my messenger bag in my locker and took out my English book and notebook. With everyone who passed me—the halls were full of students—I hoped no one would say anything about Friday. Mom had assured me that morning over Apple Jacks that everyone would have forgotten the whole thing by today.

"Oh, hey. I was at Arlene's house. Remember? For the Academy Awards," I said. There had been a message from Kirstie on my pillow when I got home late from Arlene's. I was surprised when I saw that she had called. I figured she'd have forgotten about me over the weekend. I felt like a little social butterfly, even, getting messages from one person while I was out with another. Sad, right?

"I remember. But you were there all night? Saturday and Sunday?" She squeezed her notebook to her chest, and the way her eyes pierced me made me nervous—like I was being questioned by the principal.

"No," I said, wondering why she was questioning me like I'd done something wrong. "I just got home late. The awards ended at, like, eleven thirty."

"Oh," she said. "That's cool. Hey!" she said, brightening. "Can we meet before lunch? Friday I roamed the halls because I was afraid to go in and sit alone."

"You did? Of course I'll meet you. Arlene and I usually meet in courtyard just outside the caf. Meet us there and we'll all go in together."

As my morning classes went on, I had to think that maybe Mom had been right. Maybe everyone did forget about the roses. Still, I was on alert in case anyone tried any other pranks on me like Kirstie said she'd overheard. I couldn't help but think she was wrong about that. I don't think she was lying or anything, but she was brand-new here—how would she know who anyone was talking about? By lunch, I started to relax.

I introduced Kirstie to Arlene, and we went inside the caf and got in line. While Arlene was getting her food, Kirstie nudged me and said, "She looks familiar." I didn't know what that meant or what to tell her, so I just shrugged my shoulders.

As I paid for the lasagna and "green" beans, Lunchlady Campbell smiled and said, "Oh, Sara! I saw your beautiful white roses in the office on Friday. You must have done some-thing special to get such gorgeous flowers."

At the day's first mention of the roses, I felt my shoulders sink. I looked straight through her thick glasses, circa before I was born, and said, "Yeah. I got my period."

She gawked for a moment, gave a shifty smile, and handed me my change.

I felt Kirstie's hand rubbing my back, and felt a tiny bit of comfort in that gesture. Arlene was in the lunchroom already, holding her tray and laughing with some softball girls. When Kirstie and I came up to her, she told the girls, "Oh. I have to go sit with them." Not for the first time, I felt like Arlene was making a huge sacrifice by sitting with me at lunch.

"You don't have to," Kirstie said, surprising me. I wasn't sure if she wanted to sit with me alone, or if she *didn't* want Arlene there.

Arlene seemed to feel there was something to her statement too, because she said, "No. I want to."

There's no way to put a finger on tension. I just knew it was there, floating in the air between Kirstie and Arlene, and I wasn't sure why.

"So where are you from, anyway?" Arlene asked almost as soon as we sat down. Well, she didn't ask so much as snap. I furrowed my brow at her, because I didn't want to be rude.

But Kirstie didn't seem bothered. "Oh, I'm not *from* anywhere, it seems. My mom and I have lived all over the place." Kirstie told us that she and her mom had been moving from city to city for as long as she could remember. Her mom works for a big hotel chain, and she constantly has to move to different cities to help open up new branches. Her dad, she said, bailed on them both when she was in second grade and she basically hasn't heard from him since. "Except for the monthly child support and alimony checks he sends," she told us. She said her dad lives in New York, making tons of money and living with a new family.

"That's gotta be kind of hard," I said. I thought it was bad enough my dad had moved out, but at least I knew he still thought about me and missed me. I knew because he called and told me so.

"I'm used to it," Kirstie said. "I'm not saying I like it. But I have made a lot of friends along the way."

"I don't know how you make new friends every year," I said. "I wouldn't have a clue how to do it. If Ms. Harrison hadn't sat me and Arlene next to each other in first grade, I might not even have her."

"Of course you would!" Arlene said. "We'd be friends no matter what."

"That's what I think," Kirstie said. "I think that friends are meant to be just like husbands or boyfriends or whatever. You and I are meant to be friends."

She said that just to me. Not to Arlene.

"So, Kristie," Arlene began.

"It's *Kir*stie," she corrected.

I'm not saying Arlene was egging her on, but I'm pretty sure she knew what Kirstie's name was. I wondered why she was being so snotty to her. I meant what I'd said: If I were a new kid at school, I'd be petrified. I was glad to be the one person who was talking to Kirstie, and I was also glad that she was the one person besides Arlene who was talking to me. Win-win.

"Sorry. *Kir*stie. Why did you start school on a Friday? That's sort of weird. Why not just start today?"

I'd been wondering the same thing too. "Mom had to start her job on Friday because of some event that that was going on that night, so she said if she had to jump right in, then I had to too. I didn't mind, though. Friday was exciting, what with all the flowers and everything." I could feel my face turn red as I set down my lasagna-laden spork. Kirstie nudged my arm and smiled at me. Arlene looked between us. Kirstie asked her, "Hey, what class do you have just before lunch?"

"Math. Why?"

"Just wondering. Where's your class?"

Arlene sighed as if she were being asked to bus the tables. "Mr. Jenkins. He's by the language department. Why?"

"I thought I saw you on Friday, that's all." Kirstie rolled her lips in and gave the slightest shake of her head. I hadn't forgotten what she'd heard on Friday, and even though her descriptions were vague—a blonde and a brunette—it seemed like she thought something was up.

Later, before I saw Kirstie again in science class, Arlene asked, "What is *up* with that girl?"

"What do you mean?" I asked. "She's okay." The truth was, I really liked her. I liked how easy she was to get along with, and how readily she had made friends with me.

"A little clingy, don't you think? And what was up with the interrogation of me and my class schedule? Why does she care?"

"She was just making conversation. She's new here. Imagine if you had to start somewhere new and you didn't know a single person. You'd ask questions too."

"Not like hers. Look, I'm sure she's nice and all, but something about her seems off. That's all."

I tried not to pay too much attention to what Arlene said. I tried not to think about their reaction to each other at lunch, which had resulted in anything but insta-friends. I tried not to think about the flowers, even though the jokes had been few and far between today. Basically, I tried not to think at all. And it was working out for me.

Until I got to science class and Kirstie slipped me a note that read, "She's the one. Meet me by the marquee after school!"

♥ 5 ♥

Do You Stand Out from the Crowd,
or Blend In with the Scenery?

At the spring dance, you decide to be bold and try out some new
dance moves. What happens?

a) A circle forms around you, some people laughing, some cheering
you on, but soon, everyone is mimicking your stellar moves.

b) A few people around you ask if you're having an epileptic fit.

c) The dance goes on just the same.

Kirstie led me away from the school toward her house, telling
me we'd figure it all out as soon as we got to her place. And
her place was gargantuan.

It sat at the end of the cul-de-sac atop a small hill in the
swanky Sugar Hill subdivision of town. The house was red
brick with white shutters and had a half-moon porch as big
as my bedroom. The driveway swung around the side of the

house, tossed around back like a rope. Four pillars as tall as the second floor held the house up, making the porch look like a toothless grin held up by Popsicle sticks.

The glass in the front door rippled as we walked closer, making what little I could see of the interior look like it was underwater. Kirstie wrapped her fingers around the brass handle and swung the door open.

"Come in to my lair," she said, looking at me with exaggerated wide eyes. Despite the unnerving situation, I sort of laughed and stepped inside, eager to see how big it was and what it looked like. I wondered if they had an entire game room, maybe an indoor bowling alley.

Kirstie pulled off her boots and dropped them beside a pair of red satin strappy heels and Nike tennis shoes. I did the same, figuring it was a rule. Wasn't this an Asian thing, taking off your shoes?

"Hello?" she hollered, then stood quietly, listening for an answer. "Mother must still be at work. Probably staying late to impress her new bosses. Come on." She took my hand, then softly dropped it, sending an unexpected zing through me. She led me down a carpeted hallway as white as piano keys—probably the reason for the no-shoes thing. "Let's go to my room and hash out a war plan," she said, leading me up a long, curved stairwell.

Upstairs, Kirstie plopped down on her bed, which was red and bigger than my mom's and cluttered with makeup, hairspray, and old copies of *Cosmopolitan*. "Let's think about this rationally. Why would your *best friend*," she said, finger-quoting the last two words, "do this to you?"

"I don't know. Are you sure it was Arlene?" I asked for the millionth time since leaving school.

Kirstie looked at me sadly. "I'm sorry. But I'm sure."

I dropped my messenger bag by the door and sat in a desk chair chipped with lime green paint. Her room was crammed with moving boxes, mostly unopened but a few with clothes hanging limply over the sides. Kirstie looked at me as if we had always been friends, like we had just had a sleepover last weekend. I had been flattered at first that someone was paying so much attention to me and seemed so concerned for me, but I started to wonder what her angle was.

I tugged on the thighs of my jeans and asked, "Why have you been so nice to me? You don't even know me. Maybe I'm a huge jerk."

She sighed. "I know you're not a jerk. And I completely know what it's like to be in a situation like this, and I know that I would have liked it if someone had helped me along."

"Oh." I wondered what had happened to her, but figured if she wanted to tell me, she would.

We sat quietly for a moment, then Kirstie said, "Maybe Arlene and that girl were just talking. If you think about it, it doesn't make sense, anyway. What would anyone have to gain by doing something like that? Honestly, it sounds like more trouble than it's worth, dragging in that huge box of Kotex. The one doing it might get caught with the box herself."

"I guess," I said. "She's innocent until proven guilty, right?"

It seemed like a dumb thing to say, but Kirstie said, "Exactly! It's not even worth bringing up to her. Just wait and see if anything happens, because I bet nothing will. I'm sure she'll prove me wrong."

"Yeah," I said, but I didn't feel confident about anything—whether Arlene was up to something, whether Kirstie was mistaken, or whether I was just reading into things too much. I didn't know what to think or feel about any of it, but I didn't want to freak out either. "Besides, before I start to worry if there's going to be some joke played on me, I'm a little freaked out that word got out about them, anyway. I only told one person about it."

"Arlene?" she guessed, her eyebrows hovering high above her traffic-light eyes.

I gulped. "Yes. But she wouldn't tell anyone." Despite myself, I added, "I don't think."

"Oh," Kirstie said, looking down at her red bedspread. "Look, Sara. I don't know Arlene and I certainly don't know your friendship. But if she's really your best friend, then she wouldn't do anything. Right?"

"Right." I shook my head. "This is stupid. Maybe I should just ask her. She'll be honest with me."

"Maybe," Kirstie said, although she looked doubtful. Another pang rushed through my stomach.

"Anyway," I began, not wanting to talk about it anymore. Nothing bad like this had ever happened to me and Arlene. We never got in spats—we rarely even got mad at each other. The only time I really got mad at her was when she cancelled our Razzie night in October, but I never said anything to Arlene, and after so long, it wasn't worth mentioning, even if it still irked me. Wanting to change the subject, I asked, "What was your last school like?"

"My last school was awesome," Katie began, suddenly animated. "We were in Raleigh. It was small, private, elite—my first and only private school so far. I had the best friends in the universe. But it took one awful experience to realize how important having good friends is. The first time I moved to a new school was a nightmare."

"What happened?"

"It was terrible," she began. "We had to move to Wyoming, and the kids just did not like me. Everyone had formed their little cliques in, like, preschool, and they weren't keen on letting outsiders in. I spent the whole year there with hardly any friends. Only one girl was nice to me. And she's partly the reason I wanted to help you out. I know what it's like to be the weirdo no one wants to talk to. I think friends should always have each other's backs."

It was comforting, if a bit odd, knowing that I had a new friend. I didn't like feeling like I was trading one friend in for another, but I was tired of relying on Arlene for my own entertainment. I wondered if she was sick of me, what with all her new softball friends. Was the Razzie thing just a pity party for me?

"What crowds do you usually hang out in?" I asked.

"It depends on the school. Also on me, and how I act. At my last school, I guess you could say I was in the popular crowd."

"Really?"

"Yeah. It's almost embarrassing. I was actually voted Most Popular."

"Seriously? And you were only there for one year?" I asked. "That's amazing. Here, we call it Class Favorite, but it's the same thing." In fact, it was like being a school celebrity. You got two pages of pictures in the yearbook, including fun candid shots, whereas everyone else—Most Academic, Most Versatile, etc.—only got half a page. There wasn't a ceremony announcing your win or anything, but I'd always wondered what picture day was like. All those popular and accomplished people gathered in one place, dressed up nicer than in their school picture. I wondered if they served cheese and Cokes while everyone waited their turn.

"It's no big deal," Kirstie said. "It's not like I won the Nobel Prize, just some dumb award."

"Maybe," I mumbled. I thought about Haden Prescott and her Academy Award nomination. "You know Haden Prescott, the actress?"

"From *The Silent Widow*? Sure. She didn't have a chance at the Oscar, but how pretty was she in that golden gown?"

"Amazing," I said. "Did you know she was also voted for a Golden Raspberry?" When Kirstie gave me a confused look, I said, "It's this spoof award thing for the worst movies and acting and stuff. The anti-Oscars."

"Ah."

"Anyway, when I was watching the Academy Awards this year, I couldn't believe how Haden Prescott had been a laughingstock a few months earlier with *Demon's Lover*."

"Oh, my God, how bad did that movie look?" Kirstie said.

"I know! And then she does *The Silent Widow* and everyone thinks she's brilliant. I've just been thinking, maybe I could do that."

"What, act?"

"No, turn it around. From Razzie to Oscar, or the laughingstock of Valentine's Day to Class Favorite nominee." I paused, trying to gauge her reaction. Arlene had said that Haden Prescott proved that any loser could turn it around, and I wondered if Kirstie would agree.

She merely shrugged her shoulders.

"Think about it," I continued. "She didn't even win, but

now she's taken as seriously as Meryl Streep. I think it's the same with Class Favorite. Like, people respect you more. They don't laugh at you and tease you. As it is now, my school will remember me as the baby who got roses from her mother for getting her period. Not to mention all the other ridiculous things I do to make a fool of myself."

"I guess," she said, clearly unsure. "I'm not totally sure about the Academy Awards connection, but you can at least go for a Class Favorite nomination. There's still a couple of months left before the end of the year. Maybe just going for the nomination will make you act more confident—even if you don't feel like you are. Then, people will take you more seriously. Fame and fortune will follow," she added.

"Maybe," I said, my confidence already beginning to waver. "But what am I supposed to do? Put up a bunch of posters and hand out buttons?"

"No, look," she said, sitting up on her knees. "You just have to"—she cocked her head—"fake confidence. Do yourself up. Be like them. In all the schools I've gone to, I've learned that there are certain characteristics all popular people have across the entire country. Like poise, or who you date. I guess it's kind of the same with movie stars. You got a boyfriend?"

"No." Of course, I immediately thought of Jason. He wasn't the most popular guy in school. In fact, he used to be pretty much like me—neither here nor there. But since he made the basketball team, he was hanging out with people like Richie Adams and Sean Hurley, upping his status. I wondered why hanging out with Arlene, who was somewhere in the middle of the social food chain, hadn't done much for me.

"Then what about a crush?" Kirstie asked, plopping back down on her stomach.

"Well, actually . . ."

"Aha! You must tell!"

"It's embarrassing. You don't even know him."

"I might. Who is he? Class president? Quarterback of the football team?" She stared back at me and waited, kicking her feet behind her like she was on a kickboard in the Wave Pool at Wet 'n Wild.

"Fine. His name is Jason Andersen," I confessed, feeling the hot flush on my cheeks from saying his name.

"Okay, that's a start. What else? He's probably completely gorgeous, right?"

"Oh, my gosh, totally," I said, feeling the words ready to tumble out of my mouth. "I mean, you might not think he's good-looking, but I think he is. He has these clear hazel eyes, and he's all tall and lanky. He plays basketball, but he's not a dumb jock."

"So what are you going to do about him? You love him, right?" She grinned.

"I don't love him!"

She laughed and I couldn't help but smile with her. "Seriously, what's the game plan for this guy?"

"I don't know. Maybe a satanic cult will kidnap me and he'll come to my rescue?" All I had done so far was let my mouth drag on the ground every time he passed me in the halls. I loved watching him at his locker as he and Richie talked about plays and the previous night's game. I loved English class because I could stare at the back of his head without anyone knowing I was totally lusting.

Kirstie said, "You gotta have a goal if you want to go out with this guy. Even if your goal is to just walk up to him, tell him he's completely beautiful, then walk away mysteriously. I know! We could make up a list of things that make popular people popular, and you just make sure you do those things. The nomination will just fall into your lap then."

"A list like . . . what? What did you do at your last school that I can do too?" I asked.

"Hmmm, good question," she said, grinning happily at me. "Okay, so, I guess I would start by glaming myself up. Not that you're not gorgeous already, but you could benefit by stepping it up a notch." I tried not to cringe, looking down at my standard-issue jeans and nondescript top. "A little lip gloss goes a long way. And then, infiltrate this Jason's world. Sit where he sits at lunch. Find out where he hangs out, then we'll start hanging out there. Make him notice you."

"I don't know. Sounds kind of pathetic—like stalking."

"It's not pathetic," she defended. "What's wrong with wanting him to like you, wanting other people to like and respect you? So you want people to dig you for being something other than a period-obsessed spaz. Who cares? Why do you think there're so many movies about being popular in school? It's like, part of our genetic code. There's no avoiding it."

I thought about that. I guess there was some truth there.

"What about basketball?" Kirstie continued. "Since you don't play, do girls do anything else for the guys' teams? I don't know, like give them water or something?"

"Oh, man, that's it." It was so brilliant. "Stat girl!"

"What's that?"

"They're the girls who write the statistics for the players. You know, how many baskets a guy makes, how many free throws, fouls, stuff like that. They have them all year, for all the sports. Stat girls get to hang out with the guys through every practice and every game. They're like part of the team. You know what?" I paused, thinking. "This one girl did stats until the girls' team complained that they needed her more. Her slot might still be open."

"So there it is. Do that. How do you get to be one? Isn't the season almost over?"

"Yeah. There's only a few more games left, I think." I thought for a moment and then remembered. "I could ask my sister. She and Coach Eckels are super tight. She still asks for his advice on, like, a weekly basis. Maybe I could ask her if she could ask him?"

"That's so cool you have a sister you can turn to when you need stuff," Kirstie said, tearing the edges of a *Cosmo*. "My mom is cool and all, but sometimes I wish I had a little sister to take care of."

"Humph." I thought about all the times my sister had sat on me and farted, or asked me to hang out in her room, then shut the door in my face. "Believe me, I'd rather be an only child any day."

"You only say that because you don't know what it's like to be alone."

"I guess." I thought for a moment. Then I said, "And you're only saying so because you don't know otherwise."

She laughed and said, "Okay. How about this: When we hang out, you can pretend like you're an only child and I'll pretend that you're my little sister. I can help you with things like getting hooked up with Jason Andersen and making Class Favorite. What do you say?"

She looked at me with a hopeful gleam in her eyes. Maybe it was completely horrible being an only child. Sure, I hated Elisabeth and all that stuff, but we did play together when we were kids. She had even given me some advice over the years.

"Yeah," I said. "Sounds cool."

✳✳✳

Having a goal seemed like the productive thing to do. So, as soon as I got home, I decided to start right in on my Class Favorite–nominee quest before I could even think about what I was doing.

I saw Elisabeth sitting on her bed through her half-open door, her long, tanned legs bent as she painted her toenails cotton candy pink. I stuck my head through the door and asked, "Can I come in?"

She glanced up. "I guess."

Elisabeth's room was always spotless, despite being cluttered with running trophies. She even made her bed in the mornings without Mom telling her to. At the edge of her bed was a copy of *Running* magazine, her biology textbook, a red folder, and her diary. She had a copy of *Us Weekly* under her foot to keep any nail polish from getting on her comforter.

I sat on the floor facing her, my back up against the wall next to her tennis shoes, my legs straight out in front of me.

"You're so lucky Mom doesn't humiliate you," I began, referring to the flowers.

"She didn't mean to," she said. It was just like her to be the good daughter, even when Mom wasn't around to notice.

"It's so embarrassing," I said. "I'm surprised you didn't hear about it over at your school."

"I can't believe you're still worrying about that. Listen."

She screwed the cap back on the polish and set it on her nightstand. "I totally agree that what happened on Friday was humiliating, but it wasn't Mom's fault—she was just trying to be nice. And you said you already got teased for it. I'm sure everyone's moved on from it by now. You should too."

"Maybe," I said. "I just wish I knew how everyone found out." I looked up at my sister and asked, "A school administrator could get fired for telling stuff about a student, right?"

"What are you talking about?"

"Never mind."

Elisabeth leaned back against her headboard, gave me a look, and said, "Sara, if you want something, just ask."

"Well, I was wondering if you'd do me a favor."

"Obviously."

"I'm just trying to think of ways to make my life a little easier. So I was just wondering, you know, since you're such good friends with Coach Eckels, and since he's the guys' basketball coach and you're so close to him and all, will you please, next time you see him, ask him if I can be a stat girl? *Please?*"

"Why don't you ask him yourself?"

"Because he likes you."

She picked up a bottle of clear polish and rhythmically slapped it on her palm.

"Why didn't you tell me you started your period?" she suddenly asked.

"Why did you have to out me to Mom about it?" I retorted.

"Sara, you make too big a deal of things."

"Oh, right. Like having guys offer me a tampon is no big deal." I felt like no one understood what had happened. The worst thing that had ever happened to Elisabeth was the time she came in second in the 1,600-meter, and that was only because she was getting over the flu.

"Getting your period isn't a big deal. Don't let them make you think it is. They're just being immature."

"It's just so humiliating having everyone know when I got it. Besides, why do you even care?"

"Sara," she said, looking down at me. "I'm your *sister*."

She didn't state it like it was the obvious, though. More like she just wanted to let me know that there were some things she would always be there for.

"So will you talk to Coach Eckels for me?"

She slowly opened the bottle, then continued with steady strokes across each toe, her chin resting on her knee. A heavy silence filled the room, one that I was pretty sure Elisabeth created for the sole purpose of torturing me with anticipation. It worked.

She exhaled dramatically, and I prepared for my boring days to change—or to stay the same way for eternity.

"Fine," she finally said. "But you owe me."

♥ 6 ♥

Do You Know Who You Can Trust?

You really need to talk to your best friend about the latest development in the ongoing saga of your love life, but she's not at school today. Instead, there's Veronica, a relatively new girl you've become friendly with. What do you do?

a) Tell her your problem, automatically assuming that she'll keep the information mum.

b) Tell her your problem, but make her swear on her cat's life that she won't tell a soul.

c) Wait and call your best friend when you get home—you'd rather not take the risk.

In English class the next morning, I couldn't even look at Arlene. I felt sick to my stomach with worry, thinking that maybe, just maybe, she was out to get me. Despite Kirstie's advice to just leave it alone, I really wanted to ask her if she was planning on pulling any little pranks on me. I was sure she'd tell me she didn't know what I was talking about—and would mean it. Still, our lack of any kind of confrontation or miscommunication over the years had left me not knowing exactly how to approach her. So, I stalled. I didn't even wait for her outside the caf like I normally do.

Holding my lunch tray, I stood before the half-filled tables, people talking and laughing, and the occasional fry flying across a table. I saw Jason Andersen's table, which was completely full but for one seat . . . right next to him. To his left was Jessica, who had movie star–blond hair and dated Richie Adams; she and Kayla were laughing with their heads close together. Jason sat quietly, almost alone in the midst of the chaos of the lunchroom table. I thought of what Kirstie had said about sitting at his lunch table and faking confidence. For a daring moment I considered just plopping down at that one empty seat next to him and saying, "So, whaddaya think of that book we're reading in English? You ready for the game next week?" I wondered how Jason and the others at the table would react.

Maybe I should try it, I thought. I was looking pretty okay that day. When I woke up that morning, instead of stressing over Arlene, I thought about Class Favorite-dom. With the stat girl thing from Elisabeth in the works, I decided to glam myself up, like Kirstie had suggested. I snagged Elisabeth's powder, mascara, and lip gloss from her makeup bag while she was in the shower and did my best to apply it all correctly. As soon as I had gotten the mascara on both eyes—after stabbing my eyeball twice—I promptly sneezed, squeezing my eyes and smearing mascara all over my upper and lower eyes. I had to quickly scrub it all off and start over again before Elisabeth got out of the shower, and then I had to keep my head down and avoid looking at her or my mom for the rest of the morning. Trying to be pretty was very exhausting.

Just as I lifted my Ked-clad foot to walk over to Jason's table, Richie Adams came through the open doors of the cafeteria and sat next to Jason, slapping him on the back as he took that last seat. So much for my few seconds of bravery.

After I'd stood holding my tray long enough to look weird, I glared toward the FFA table. Ellen wasn't there, but the other girls and guys were, all in Wranglers and Rocky Mountains, big belt buckles and Ropers. The girls probably spent Saturday nights discussing cow feed while not washing their hair, I thought bitterly. But maybe that was better than staying home alone.

I took a deep breath and started toward the FFA table.

"Sara, wait up," Arlene called from behind me.

For a brief moment I was glad to have been stopped. I felt that if I sat with the FFA kids, nice as I'm sure they were, I'd never be seen as the sophisticated woman who was on her way to Class Favorite glory. I still wasn't exactly sure how I was going to achieve my nomination goal, but I was pretty sure it didn't involve cows and goats.

I turned to face Arlene, my lunch tray heavy in my hands. Her blond hair was tucked behind her ears, and her cheeks had a fresh, rosy tint to them. My heart raced.

"What?" she asked. When I didn't say anything—I was trying to think of *what* to say—she said, "I was waiting outside for you. How come you didn't wait for me?"

She'd been my best friend for so long, and I really loved her, but when she wanted to know why *I* wasn't waiting on *her*, I got angry. I'm not sure if I was angry at myself for not having more friends, or angry at her for expecting me to always be around. I had so many conflicting emotions swirling around my head as it was, and when she stood before me, acting like I needed to wait on her, I just snapped. There was no equality in our friendship, I thought. It was always me following her, or waiting on her to grace me with her presence.

"Why should I always have to wait on you?" I heard myself say.

Arlene looked taken aback. "You don't," she said. "But your class is closer to the caf than mine."

"Well, maybe I'm tired of waiting around on you while you take your time, chatting with all your little friends along the way."

"What's wrong with you? Are you mad at me about something?"

Friends have fights, I told myself. I was allowed to be angry with her if I wanted to be. And I certainly had the right to confront her. I tried to keep my confidence up when I asked, straight up, "Did you tell anyone about the roses, Arlene?"

"The roses? From Friday? You're still thinking about those?"

"I asked you a question," I said, and I have to shamefully admit that seeing her look so confused and even a little scared made me feel that much more in control even though, deep down, I was more afraid of losing Arlene than anything else. "You swore to me you wouldn't tell anyone."

"You think *I* told people about them?"

"No, I don't. I don't think you told anyone about it, just like you didn't tell anyone about my basketball tryout disaster."

"Wait, this is too random. First of all, the basketball tryout thing wasn't exactly a secret—there were fifty other girls there."

"I told you not to tell my sister, and you did."

"Secondly," she forced, "I already apologized for that. I really didn't think it was a big deal." Arlene took a deep breath. In a calm voice she said, "Look. I know Friday was awful, and I'm really sorry. The truth is, no one even cares anymore. Most people care more about who didn't get flowers. Did you hear that Richie sent Jessica *carnations*? They say she's thinking of breaking up." I glared at her, and she said, "You're totally overreacting. Those flowers are so over."

"That's easy for you to say. Everything's been working out perfectly for you since we left elementary school."

Arlene huffed and said, "What exactly are we talking about?"

"You and your big mouth. You can't keep anything a secret. You gossip with people just to get them to like you—like all those loser softball girls."

Arlene shook her head and said, "I've never done anything mean, Sara, and you know it."

"When it's not happening to you, I guess I could see how having the entire school knowing my private business isn't anything mean. It's not like you're the one who has to sit through class while people throw tampons at your head." I slightly exaggerated on that last bit, but Friday's algebra class didn't feel far from that.

"Look," she said, clearly more annoyed than sympathetic. "I'm really sorry about Friday. I'm sorry some immature jerks were mean to you. And I'm sorry your mother sent you roses that happened to come from my mother's shop. If you were so upset with *me* over all this, I wish you would have just said something."

I gritted my jaw and shifted the lunch tray I still held in my now-sweaty hands. I was angry that Arlene was angry, but at the same time, I knew this was more than just a spat between friends. Testing the state of our friendship, I said, "Do you want to come over on Friday and watch the new Razzie worst picture winner? You said you wanted to see it before our regular Saturday night thing."

Arlene looked off toward the athletes' table; some girl whose name I didn't know waved at her. She looked at me and said, "You know I have games on Fridays. Maybe I can come over after. . . ."

"Forget it," I said quickly. "I don't even care."

"Look." Arlene's eyes began turning dark. "I've already apologized to you for about ten things. I said I was sorry for things I didn't even do. What's your problem?" She stood, defiant, waiting for an answer.

"You are."

"We're supposed to be best friends," she said.

"Exactly."

"Well, if we are," she said, her voice rising, "then I'd think you'd believe your own *best friend* when she tells you she didn't tell anyone about your stupid period flowers!"

"God, Arlene, I don't think the cooks in the back of the kitchen heard you!"

"Sara, are you okay?" asked a voice from behind us. We both turned to see Kirstie standing just off to the side, her thin arms folded over her stomach. She walked toward us but kept her eyes on Arlene. The sort of comfort Kirstie's presence gave me right then was exactly what I needed.

"It's okay," I told Kirstie.

"Well, look who it is," Arlene said, and I hated the accusing tone in her voice.

"Yeah, look who it is," I said to Arlene. "My friend."

"What's that supposed to mean?" Arlene's eyes were filled

with confusion. I stared back at her, trying not to cry.

"Let's go, Sara," Kirstie finally said, taking my tray and dropping it on a nearby table. She gave my arm a tug and guided me out of the barfeteria. I wanted to look back at Arlene. But I didn't.

"Just forget about her."

That's the advice Kirstie had for me when she called me that night. The truth was, I was completely shaken up by the whole encounter with Arlene. I'd never spoken to Arlene— or anyone—like that before. I don't think I believed half the things I'd said to her. All I had really wanted to do was ask her if she had any pranks planned against me, and it'd all gotten so out of control that I hadn't even asked her the one thing I wanted to know. I was embarrassed by how immaturely I had handled myself, and how I'd treated my best friend. More than anything, I was confused by what I felt and what I believed.

"If you were my best friend," Kirstie continued, "I'd never break your confidence. Not even once. I didn't even really think she was the one who had spread the word, but if she's the only one you confided in, that pretty much speaks volumes. Don't you think?"

My mind was wandering, but when I realized she expected a response, I pulled myself out of it. "Yeah, I guess," I muttered. I'd been sulking in my room since dinner and didn't plan on coming out until the next morning. I wished that Elisabeth was the kind of sister I could talk to about this stuff, but since she was never home it wasn't worth trying. Mom was always around, but between her and Dad, Dad was easier to talk to. If he still lived here I could probably find him out back inspecting the yard. It was just so hard trying to process what was happening with Arlene, and I couldn't imagine a world where she and I wouldn't be friends—and, worse, one in which she could screw me over big-time. I guess nothing felt right lately.

"I'm really sorry about the whole mess," Kirstie continued. "You can always call me if you need anything."

"I know," I said. "Thanks." Even in my daze, I still wondered why Kirstie was being so nice to me. The truth was, with everything in shambles, Kirstie was all I had. I decided to not read anything into her friendly gestures.

"Oh! How could I forget," she said suddenly. "Next week for spring break, Mother is taking me to Aspen and said I can invite a friend. And since you're pretty much my only friend, it'd be so fun if you came. We'll even pay."

I should have been flattered, but the truth was, Kirstie and I barely knew each other—our friendship seemed to be moving pretty quickly. Besides, Arlene and I had planned a marathon viewing of Razzies for the break—we already had five movies picked out, but with what had happened, I could forget that now. Maybe going on a trip with a new friend wasn't such a bad idea. Plus, I secretly thought, having some exotic travel stories would make me seem like a woman of the world. Very Class Favorite-ish.

"Wow." I tried to force enthusiasm into my voice. "Totally. I'll ask my mom."

"The best remedy for a broken heart is distance," Kirstie said. I got the feeling that, in all her moving from place to place, it was something she knew a lot about.

Over the next couple of days, Arlene tried to call me a few times, but seeing her number on my caller ID, I ignored it. It was hard to know what to say when I still didn't know what to believe. Every time I told myself she hadn't leaked word, I reminded myself that she was the only one who knew—and that she had told stuff about me in the past. Still, the thought of our friendship being ruined for good always sent my mind reeling.

Soon, Arlene began ignoring me too, and I took her silence as guilt. I didn't want to stay mad at Arlene forever, but every time I saw her, she seemed to be having so much fun with her other friends that I realized she wasn't even missing me. Her ease at forgetting me—at not even needing me—really burned. I didn't know whether to be hurt or just plain angry. I was glad to have Kirstie around. At least I wasn't lonely.

I decided that since Arlene was obviously upping her status in school with her athletic friends, I would finally try to move out of wallflower-dom and get some good recognition. I decided to talk more to Kirstie about making the Class Favorite list—maybe she could help me come up with a real, concrete plan of how one could go from nothing to something in a matter of a couple of months. We never did make that list we had talked about for Class Favorite qualities, but I wanted to do it.

Sometimes I wonder what the heck I was thinking.

Do You Have What It Takes
to Be the Coolest Kid in Class?

Which word best describes your attitude toward popularity?

a) superficial

b) (my) reality

c) unachievable

It had been more than a week since my lunchroom confrontation with Arlene, and we had become experts at avoiding each other. We didn't look at each other in class, and I sat with Kirstie at lunch. I slowly began to think that Arlene wasn't going to pull some locker prank on me, and I began to feel like maybe I'd made a huge mistake. I'd been so embarrassed about the flowers that I was afraid I'd taken it out on her. And yeah, it's true that I felt left out, what with all her new friends. But that didn't mean she'd betray me, even if she secretly didn't consider me her best friend anymore.

"I think I'm going to talk to Arlene," I told Kirstie one evening when we were at her house making root beer floats and watching E!. "She hasn't done anything to me. No locker pranks, nothing." I stirred the long spoon in my frosted mug. "I think it's time to grovel."

"You think that's a good idea?" she asked, surprising me. "I'm just thinking . . . maybe she's waiting for the storm to settle, and then she's going to do something."

"I don't think so. I think that, even if she was going to do something at one point, she's not planning on doing it anymore. I think the storm hasn't just settled—it's passed."

Kirstie dipped her spoon into her float thoughtfully. "Maybe just wait until after spring break before you say anything to her—just to make sure. I have to be honest—I have a bad feeling about the whole thing. So wait a little longer. For me?"

I hesitated before I said, "Yeah, sure." Even though I wasn't sure. I felt confused and saddened about Arlene, and torn with Kirstie, who had been the only person there for me since Valentine's Day, it seemed. Now everything was all turned around and upside down.

Every time I saw Arlene she really looked like she'd moved on quite easily. It hurt my feelings knowing she could go on as if we were never friends. Still, I told myself, despite what Kirstie said, I'd make a sort of last-ditch effort and apologize. I thought it was the right thing to do.

That night when I got home from Kirstie's, I shuffled down the hall to the room that used to be Dad's office but was now just a tiny junk storage room. A dusty desk with our one computer sat in front of the window that faced out the side of the house. Mom had gotten our computer free from the bank when they upgraded, and it was such a piece of junk that it groaned and wheezed every time we turned it on. I couldn't even IM because it always crashed, so I had to make do with regular ol' e-mails, but I guess it was okay.

When the computer finally groaned to life I froze. I had an e-mail from Arlene:

First of all, I told myself I wasn't going to write you for a while after what you said to me in the lunchroom that day. I wanted to cool off and think about things. I actually tried to see things from your perspective. But the more I thought, the angrier I got. How could you accuse me of doing something without even hearing me out first?? I don't know who told about your flowers, but I do know who was in the office when they came: your new "friend" Kirstie. She really leeched on to you pretty quickly. Did you ever stop to wonder why?

That was it. That's how the e-mail ended. I didn't know how to respond, or even if I should. I thought about calling

Kirstie, but I didn't. I wanted to think about how I would respond, so I closed the e-mail, telling myself I'd answer it later. But I never got the chance.

Since it was the week before spring break, a buzz filled the air—talk in the halls became louder and more excited, people laughed more often, and everyone, even the teachers, seemed like they were in a good mood. A little joy had even seeped into me, despite my situation with Arlene.

Miracle of all miracles, Mom had agreed to let me go skiing with Kirstie and her mom. She only had two conditions: We would pay my way, and she insisted on speaking with Kirstie's mom before we left. So far, they'd been playing phone tag, but I wasn't worried—I was too excited. Kirstie let me borrow an old pair of ski pants, and her mom said I could borrow her jacket ("It gives me an excuse to buy a new one," she'd said).

But because this is my miserable life, when I got to algebra, Mrs. Everly, who has been a teacher since before the abacus was invented, announced we were having a pop quiz on systems of equations, even though we had just started studying them. I rolled my eyes and thought how perfect this was.

Mrs. Everly handed a stack of test papers to the person at the front of each row, licking her finger as she counted them out. I was glad that I sat four seats back—hopefully by the time the papers got to me, her spit would be dry. Old people can be so disgusting.

"You have twenty minutes," she ominously announced.

It was just like her to give a quiz right before spring break, when no one wanted to do anything but talk about where they were going and what they were doing. Sometimes you had to wonder if teachers have any memory of what it was like to be a student. I stared down at my sheet and tried to focus. I decided to give a halfhearted attempt, knowing that Mrs. Everly throws out our lowest quiz score for each six-week period.

Once I decided to suck on the quiz, my eyes started to wander. Everybody's head was down on their sheets, including Mrs. Everly's, who was probably doing the crossword puzzle in the back of *Woman's Life*. I don't think she really gave her classes much thought anymore, especially since nothing new ever happens in the world of math. It's been the same nonsense for a hundred years.

Jason sat by the window, his long back rounded over his paper. His smooth-skinned face was fixed in concentration, and I realized I had no idea what kind of grades he made. Must have been average, considering he wasn't in honors algebra. Kayla Cane, whose almond-colored hair always rested perfectly on her back, had probably never had an unpopular day in her life. I looked over at Rosemary Vickers, who sat in the front row on the far right, next to the door. Her thick mane of red hair had hundreds of shiny gold strands mixed in, making it shimmer even in the dull fluorescent lights of the classroom. I fingered my own hair, so thin that my sister teased that I'll have bald spots by the time I graduate high school.

Rosemary tucked her locks behind her ear with French-manicured nails and tapped her bright blue pencil on her desk. She wasn't athletic, and she was still popular. I wondered how she did it. Yeah, she was nice and really pretty, but what made her seem so great to everyone? She wasn't the only nice, pretty girl in town. She dated, but hadn't had a boyfriend since last year. Not because she couldn't get one—she obviously just chose to stay single.

I rested my chin in the palm of my hand, even though I read in *Seventeen* that the dirt from your hand gives you zits, and wondered what it *was* about her that made everyone like her so much. Every girl who had been nominated for Class Favorite had great hair, and they all had nice nails—whether they were short or long, they were always manicured. I'd painted my nails a pale pink from a home manicure kit, but it didn't look near as nice as Rosemary's or Kayla's. I'd never seen Rosemary get in a fight with anyone, and I never heard of anyone being angry with her. I watched as she scratched her freckled forehead, then gazed around the room. She looked back at me, and before I realized I had been staring at her, she smiled and shrugged her shoulders, and I somehow knew it had to do with the quiz. I smiled and rolled my eyes as she turned back around. My heart thumped in my chest.

I'd never had one of the popular kids acknowledge me before, except that time I accidentally sneezed on Kayla Cane in the halls earlier this year. She got this totally disgusted look on her face and screeched, "Ew! Gross!"—which is normal when you've had snot spewed on you by a stranger. Her friend Jessica laughed and said to me, "Way to go, grace." Kayla, though, was not amused. She held out the arm I'd blown spit and snot on, wiped it on my shirt, and snapped, "You're nasty."

So all popular girls weren't nice, and having Rosemary acknowledge me in algebra was almost as exciting as having Jason himself engage in a full-on conversation with me, I decided.

"Time's up," Mrs. Everly announced. "Everyone pass your papers forward."

I looked down at my sheet. I had barely answered half.

Twenty minutes later, Mrs. Everly went over all the questions on the quiz and I realized that, even with the questions I had gotten around to answering, I had only successfully answered the first three problems correctly. *Screw it,* I thought as the bell rang and we all slapped our books shut. I glanced at Rosemary, who dropped her blue pencil in her red Coach as I slipped on my tan corduroy jacket. Richie passed her and said,

"Later, Rose," and she smiled at him. Jason tapped his pencil on her head and winked at her. I deliberately stuffed my book and papers into my faded black messenger bag, trying to keep pace with her. Whatever it was that Rosemary had, I wanted a piece of it.

I thought back to that recent night at Kirstie's, when she finally helped me make the list of all the things that made popular people popular, like we had talked about. I would use it to tick off qualities for my Class Favorite quest, as well as to see how people like Rosemary made it to the top every year. Kirstie'd already given me pointers about my outward appearance—she suggested I cut my hair in long, sweeping layers and give it some golden highlights. I'd gone to Supercuts but chickened out and just asked for a trim. I also realized I couldn't afford the color job, and still planned to buy a home-job at the grocery store. We talked more about the connection between Haden Prescott's ascent and how I could do the same. We thought of things she had, and used those as guidance for me. This is what we came up with:

1. Hotness. Duh. Every movie star, even the D-listers, are beautiful. Same with popular people. (This made me wonder a thousand other things: Am I good-looking? Is popular beauty natural, or can I acquire it? Do you have to get a professional manicure? What about a pedicure? Or only in the summer? Do

you have to get your hair done at Toni & Guy, or was Supercuts okay so long as it looked like something out of *CosmoGirl*? Was the home color job I was planning on buying okay or was it total white trash? And, wait, was *CosmoGirl* even cool, or was it so sixth grade?)

2. The clothes. They really do count, don't they? Maybe Bai Ling was a great actress, but she dressed horribly and so was never taken seriously. For me, Kirstie had suggested more skirts—short ones, she said—but I didn't have many in my arsenal. She'd loaned me a couple, but she was taller than I was and they ended up being knee-length. She promptly took them back, ordering me to the mall, *stat*.

3. Niceness. Here I got confused. Like I said, Rosemary is one of the sweetest girls in school, Kayla, not so much. Both were equally popular. Kirstie told me she was always nice, and sometimes people liked her, sometimes they thought she was a freak. "There's no way of knowing," she'd said. But I'd always been nice. Hadn't I? How did my lunchroom brawl with Arlene fit into this?

4. Boyfriend. In Hollywood, arm candy boys were always a bonus but not necessary. In Ladel, Rosemary didn't have a boyfriend, but she was probably an exception. Being the girlfriend of someone popular must be an excellent way to get your name on the CF ballots. But do you have to be popular already to get the popular guy? And in the real world of Bowie, could Jason ever be mine?

5. Poise. Even when being grilled on the Oscars red carpet about her personal life, Haden Prescott had not faltered; she graciously declined to answer such questions. Was it even possible for me to keep it together considering the levels of humility I'd been enduring since V-Day?

6. Academics. Ugh. I hoped you didn't have to be an Eric von Trieger—smartest person in our class—to be popular. Of course, Eric wasn't really popular. People sort of respected him because he did so well in school, and sometimes he tutored kids. So, is intelligence moot? Many Hollywood actors were high school dropouts, but I didn't respect that. (Hmm . . . funny reading this one as I purposely bombed my algebra quiz.)

7. Confidence. Like Kirstie said, even if I don't have any (which I don't), I should at least fake it.

8. How many friends you have! I'd lost one and gained another, but was that enough?

Leaving algebra, I took my list from my bag and got right up to Rosemary's desk just as she gathered her books. She had smiled at me during class, so I told myself there was no reason to be intimidated by her.

"Hey, Rosemary," I said enthusiastically. I kind of stood in front of her for a sec, then realized I was blocking her from getting out of the aisle. "Oh, sorry," I offered.

"That's okay," she said, glancing blankly at me with her

long-lashed eyes. I made a mental note of her nude glossy lipstick. As she stepped around me, the smell of green apples wafted past me. How could she smell so good this late in the day?

I followed her out the class door, and when she turned left she looked over her shoulder curiously to see me coming up behind her. I forced my instant fear of looking like a stalker out of my mind and focused on my first task: acting normal.

"Hey," I said again.

"Hey." She grinned, showing her pearl-white crooked front teeth, which, you know, actually looked pretty cute on her. I'd just assumed she'd had braces like everyone else . . . except me, of course.

"Hey, Kayla," she said to my spit 'n' sneeze victim, who was walking with Jessica.

"Text me!" Kayla called to Rosemary as she passed us, not even bothering to look at me.

"So," I said, glancing back at them. I pressed on. "That quiz sucked, huh?"

She gave a little "humph," like something between a laugh and a hiccup. "I guess. Hi again, Jason," she said as we passed him leaning against the lockers.

Oh, yummy Jason . . .

" 'S up, Rosemary," he said. Did he just smile at me?

"Yeah," I continued. "I hate pop quizzes," which I immediately regretted saying because who likes any sort of quizzes, much less the pop kind?

Rosemary politely stared ahead, so I quickly glanced down at my CF qualities list, then said, "Oh, hey, those are really cute jeans. Where'd you get them?"

As we got to her locker and she started spinning her combination, she started to look downright suspicious of me or maybe just annoyed. But she kept answering my questions.

"The mall," was her reply, which wasn't a really revealing answer. I mean, everything comes from the mall. But did she get it at a place like Macy's or 5.7.9?

Once she closed her locker and started back down the hall, I realized I might have time for two more questions, because she was heading in the direction of my locker, which I needed to stop by before last period. And if I left her there, it'd be like she was following me, like she was walking *me* to *my* locker, and then maybe it wouldn't look so weird. That's what I was hoping for, anyway.

"So," I said as we rounded the corner. "Got big plans this weekend?"

Up the hall, I could hear Shiner's high-pitched laugh. He shoved a sixth grader against a locker and twisted his nipple.

"Woo-hoo!" he hollered. "Go on, whistle! Whistle!"

"Ow! Come on, man!" the kid hollered as he sputtered out a whistle-less blow.

Rosemary glared toward Shiner, and I felt sorry for the kid he had in his greasy grip. "Not big plans," Rosemary answered. "Just hanging out with some friends."

"Cool. Your parents let you stay out late? 'Cause my mom, she can be a real pain sometimes about curfew. But if my dad still lived at home, I think it would be worse. Your folks still together?"

"Yeah," she answered as we headed toward my locker and the front of the building.

As we came up on my locker, we both noticed a crowd around it. I saw Rosemary's mouth fall open before my own could.

My first thought was that there had just been a fight. I imagined someone was on the floor, face beaten bloody, waiting for someone to haul him to the nurse's office before he went to the principal's. It was the look on everyone's face that made me think that: Some were laughing, some were whispering to one another, lots had their faces scrunched up in disgust, like whoever was in the center of their circle was really horrendously messed up.

Can You Exude Beauty in an Ugly Situation?

You're strutting through the food court wearing your killer new cream-colored pants, when a five-year-old menace comes racing through the aisles, smearing your pants with ketchup and mustard. How do you react?

a) By screaming at the kid for ruining your clothes and telling his mother she's an unfit parent

b) By "accidentally" tripping the kid on the way back to his table

c) By laughing it off, saying that your dull pants now look like a Jackson Pollock painting

It was an ugly, offensive mess. And it was all over *my* locker.

"That's so wrong," said student council secretary Emily Sanders.

"Oh, dude," said Sean Hurley.

"My God. Is that your locker, Sara?" Rosemary asked.

There must have been a dozen tampons taped to the outside of my locker, plus a couple of those fat, granny-size Kotex—the ones with wings, no less. My face burned hot, and I clenched my fists around the strap of my messenger bag, forcing back the tears that were threatening to burst through.

"Oh...my...God," I muttered as Rosemary stepped away from me and toward her friends, who were staring, hands over mouths. I tried to quickly think how she might handle it, but there were at least a dozen other people standing around, staring, gawking, with a tinge of pleasure on their faces—exactly the kind you get when you see a real gnarly fight. They were all whispering and shaking their heads, glancing at me but refusing to look me in the eye.

"Hey, what am I missin'?"

Shiner strutted up to the scene, textbook cupped in his hand. I took one look at him and wanted to yank that stupid coral necklace right off his chicken neck.

"What's going . . . oh man, Thurman," he said. I thought my heart would pound out of my chest and splat at his stinking feet as I waited for him to say something moronic that would add to my humiliation. But he didn't. He just stood back and stared at the ground. This was so bad that even Shiner wouldn't make fun of me.

"Who did this?" I tried to demand, but I think it came out

sounding more like a pathetic whimper with zero authority. I searched the crowd for a sign of Arlene, but she wasn't there, and I knew that if I didn't pull myself together quickly, it wouldn't be long before I started crying. My mind reeled. I was angry and embarrassed, but I had to maintain control. "Who did this?" I said again, but with more force. I didn't deserve this. I'd never done anything to anyone, and I didn't deserve to be publicly humiliated. "If no one's going to own up, either help me clean this up or just get on." I yanked a tampon off to emphasize my point, even though my hands were shaking and I felt like vomiting. When I looked back at the crowd, many were dispersing. Then I locked eyes with Jason. Of all people, he had to see this.

His hazel eyes bore into me, like he was trying to understand me. I couldn't help but stare back, thinking briefly that his eyes looked crushingly sympathetic, like when you see a dog get plowed by a Suburban. His golden-brown hair fell over his forehead, and for a microsecond I felt everything fade away. Then he gave me one of those pathetic smiles, the kind that says, *No matter how big a loser you are, we can't help but feel sorry for you.* Which made me feel even worse.

Even in the enormity of the situation, I realized I should try to exude some poise. "That was nice of them to take them out of the wrappers," I said, flicking one of the tampons.

Ugh. I immediately cringed at myself for always saying and doing the dumbest things.

Jason nodded and said, "That's one way of looking at it." And then . . . he smiled. At me. Jason Andersen looked me right in the eyes and smiled.

The warning bell rang, and everyone finally started to move on. Some last giggles, then someone joked, "Anybody got a tampon?" A few erupted in laughter.

He scratched the back of his head and looked at my locker. He sighed and said, "Man, Thurman. Whoever did this is a real psycho." He looked back at me. "Well. I guess we better get this cleaned up."

We? He said *we*? I was painfully aware that there was no *we* when it came to Sara Thurman and Jason Andersen. I stood there paralyzed, wondering what he was going to do next. I half expected him to laugh at me—"Just kidding!"—then walk away, even though I knew Jason wasn't that kind of guy.

The halls had almost completely thinned out when he set his books down on the floor, walked across the hall, and dragged a trash can over to my locker.

"Look," I said, all weak and shaky and embarrassed. "Really, you don't have to do this."

And then: *Rip!* He yanked a Kotex superabsorbent with wings off my locker and dropped it into the garbage.

"Oh, my God, Jason, I'm serious." Seeing his hands grab that winged monstrosity made everything seem wrong. Even though he might be able to help me realize my Class Favorite dreams, I didn't want him to see me like this. "Look, I'll take care of it, don't worry. This isn't your problem."

"It's not really your problem either. I mean, you didn't ask for this," he said as he tore off a tampon. Amazing that he just trusted that I didn't do something awful to deserve that. I wasn't sure I would have given the benefit of the doubt just like that.

"And if you ask me, whoever did this should totally be expelled." I couldn't handle any thought of Arlene yet. It was just too awful. Instead, I concentrated on Jason, who was actually talking to me and even sort of being my knight in shining . . . well, in a really cool Hilfiger shirt. But he probably just felt sorry for me.

And then he gave this look—a half smile with kind eyes, and then one of his blink-and-you've-missed-it winks. "Come on," he said, reaching out and lightly brushing my arm. "Let's get this mess cleaned up before Shiner comes back to take pictures or something."

He was joking, but the truth was it was a total possibility. And if anyone got a photo of this, they'd probably use the picture of my locker for my class photo instead of the one I had posed for in September.

Jason and I fell into a rhythm of tearing the taped items off and dropping them in the trash. The halls were silent, and we didn't speak, only gave fleeting glances at each other. It was actually pretty nice. Considering.

"So it's true!"

Jason and I turned to see Kirstie storming down the hall. When she got to us, she propped her hands up on her slim, curvy hips, and her mouth hung open. It was good to finally have a friend there, but it felt a little late. Anyway, weird as the situation was, I felt comfortable with Jason.

"Hey, Kirstie," I said as Jason looked over his shoulder at her, then turned back and tore some tape off my locker.

"Sara," she moaned. "You poor thing!"

"I just came out of algebra, and it was like this," I said. "This is Jason," I introduced, and then mouthed to Kirstie, *This is him!*

Jason forced some tape off his finger. "Hey," he said, looking at Kirstie briefly.

She smiled and flipped her hair off her shoulder.

I started digging my nails under the adhesive on my locker. It wasn't coming off in sheets but in little rolled-up balls. It was never going to come completely off.

"Don't you have class?" Jason asked Kirstie.

"Don't you?" she asked back.

"Yeah, I guess so." He laughed.

"Kirstie is new," I informed Jason. "She moved here from Raleigh."

"Cool," he said.

"So how'd you get stuck helping my girl here out?" she asked him.

"Volunteered."

"Wow, Sara," Kirstie said, looking to me. "You better hold on to this one. He's a keeper."

I blushed, then Jason brutally clarified, "I'm just helping out."

"You play basketball, right?" Kirstie asked him.

"Yeah. How'd you know?"

"I can tell. You just have that kind of body. Doesn't he, Sara?"

I couldn't tell if she was somehow trying to help me out or if she was hitting on him, but she was making me uncomfortable.

Kirstie reached over and pushed my hair off my face. "I can't believe this," she said. "With friends like Arlene . . ."

"I don't want to talk about it," I said, glancing at Jason.

She sighed. "Look, let's get together later and figure it out, okay? But I gotta get to history or they're going to suspend me before I get my first report card." She looked to Jason. "You headed this way?"

Jason dropped the remaining bits in the trash like a dead fish. "Yeah, I guess I should probably get to class."

"Cool, we can walk together," she said. When Kirstie looked at me, her face was both apologetic and hopeful. "You got it from here, Sar?" Kirstie asked.

"Yeah. Sure," I said, trying to sound reassuring. The aching in my stomach started creeping up again. Kirstie had talked of friends coming to each other's aid, and I wondered why she was bailing on me now. Not to mention she was taking my crush with her, even if Jason wasn't there under the most optimal circumstances. "I got this. Y'all go on."

"You sure you're okay?" Jason asked as he stepped around the trash can.

"Yeah, totally. I mean, you've done too much, anyway. Thanks a lot for helping me and all."

He did that wonderful quick-wink again and said, "No problem."

As I watched them walk down the hall, I realized that my brief interaction with Jason was a total fluke. He was just taking pity on me. And Kirstie—had she been flirting with him? Or was I being hypersensitive?

Suddenly, from far down the hall Kirstie turned to face me. Walking backward she hollered, "Polish remover!"

"What?"

"Nail polish remover! It'll help get those little stickies off your locker."

"Oh. Okay."

Alone in the quiet hallways, I dragged the trash can back to where Jason had gotten it, then tore off a bunch of blank sheets of notebook paper and covered the mess in the trash. I picked up my bag, knowing I wouldn't go to my last class. As I stood staring at my defiled locker, my shoulders started to shake, and I finally started bawling—really hard crying, the kind that makes your head hurt. I put my face in my hands, not wanting to see that stupid locker and all its disgustingness, not wanting to think that it must be Arlene who did it, or whether or not Kirstie had been flirting with Jason. I wiped my eyes, took a deep breath, and walked away.

I ran out the back entrance of the school, the breeze from my stride drying the tears on my cheeks. The leaves on the trees that surrounded the edges of the field were just beginning to bud. There was a light breeze blowing over the camouflage patches of tan and green grass on the athletic field. I whipped my hair out of my face, but the wind pushed it back. They say the weather in Texas is unpredictable, but to me, the consistency was as mind-numbingly rigid as an algebra equation. It was always cool to warm in the winter, and hotter than a hillbilly in the summer. As I headed toward the bleachers in the distance, I thought how my life was more unpredictable than Texas weather.

I turned up the collar of my corduroy jacket and stuffed my hands in my jean pockets. As I came upon the bleachers, I saw a dark figure sitting alone beneath them.

A guy squatted, smoking—I could see the little white streams of smoke. I didn't know anyone who smoked, especially not at our age. The smoker spotted me coming toward him and tossed a white bit to the ground. When I got closer, I saw that it was just Shiner.

Only one thing could come from the biggest jerk in school: pure torture. I sought solitude and found Shiner. I knew the little weasel would be ruthless, and even though I was not in the mood, I prepared myself.

"Well?" I said, looking down at him sitting on a patch of dirt. His skinny knees in baggy shorts were pulled up to his chest, and his puffy Dallas Cowboys jacket was wrapped around his bare legs.

"Well, what?"

"Well, are you hot or are you cold?"

Shiner glared back at me, and I didn't care that I was starting it this time. I mean, he *was* wearing a winter coat with shorts. He always did that, every fall and spring, and it bugged the crap out of me. Besides, I was sure that by then the whole school knew about my locker, so what did I care what Shiner thought of me?

"Leave me alone, Thurman," he mumbled, looking back down at the dirt.

"You shouldn't smoke, you know. Cancer, emphysema, bad breath . . ." When he didn't acknowledge me, I asked, "Hey, what's wrong with you?" He never let me get at him without spitting something back at me.

"I said go away. And before you start," he warned, "I didn't do that thing to your locker."

"I didn't say you did. I didn't even *think* you did."

"I'm just saying. I might do a lot of stuff, but I wouldn't do that. That was really messed up."

I sat down next to Shiner, mindful of No. 8 on my list: friends. But would he help or hurt me as a friend? Then I remembered No. 3, that I should try harder to be nice, so I settled into the dirt beside him. He ran his pale hand through his hair, and he looked tired, but not from lack of sleep— something seemed to be bugging him. I realized I hadn't been in such close proximity to him since the Fall Ball. I briefly considered that maybe he wasn't really an imbecile—maybe he just played one in our school.

"What's up with you?"

"Nothin'." He picked up a rock and tossed it past me.

"Why aren't you in class?"

"Ms. Weaver kicked me out."

"What'd you do this time?"

"I didn't do nothin'," he answered quickly.

"Yeah, right."

"It's true," he answered defensively. Shiner was always getting kicked out of class, and Ms. Weaver was notoriously evil. She once tried to have a kid expelled just for wearing a Papas and Beer T-shirt. And, one time, rumor has it, she taught school in Dallas and tried to enforce the no-hats-in-class rule on a kid named Jonathan Steinberg by making him take off his yarmulke. His parents threatened to sue the school, because of the whole freedom-from-religious-persecution thing, and Ms. Weaver dropped it, but not before Dallas could drop her. Supposedly that's how she ended up here. Kind of like a sentencing.

"You mean to tell me you were just sitting at your desk, minding your own business, and suddenly Ms. Weaver yelled at you to get the hell out of her class?"

"Pretty much."

"Come on. You were probably gleeking on someone, or making disgusting noises or gestures or *something*."

"I was not," he snapped, looking up at me. It was really a shame he had such bad skin. He might not be bad-looking if it weren't for all those red splotches on his face and neck. "She just hates me, that old witch. I didn't do anything, and she just starts hollering at me. I swear it." He grabbed another stray rock and chucked it. He gazed across the field as he took a breath, and I swear it looked like he'd been crying.

"So what happened then?" We sat facing the school—I guess so he could see if someone was coming out to bust him for skipping.

He stuffed his hands back into the pockets of his Cowboys jacket, giving me a sideways look. I don't know why, but I got the feeling he wanted me there. And not in the usual creepy Shiner kind of way.

"That dumb old woman," he began. "It's history, okay, and

we were talking about Jim Bowie and the Battle of the Alamo. All I said was that Jim Bowie was a lot like my dad. You know, 'cause they're both drunks. Ms. Weaver kind of gasps, like she can't believe I'd say such a thing about our school's freakin' namesake. But, okay, he *was* a drunk."

"Jim Bowie?"

"Yeah. And my daddy. Total alcoholics. But Ms. Weaver got so mad and said it wasn't true about either, and when I said it was so, she told me to go to the principal's office. Screw her."

"Sucks." I didn't know what else to say. What I really couldn't believe was that Shiner was saying his dad was a boozer as if he were stating that he was a car salesman. It was pretty sad to think that that was his life, but he seemed okay with it. "At least your day wasn't as bad as mine."

"Oh man, what is up with you today? Were those tampons some weird feminist statement or something?"

"Don't be stupid."

He looked me dead in the eyes and said, "Whoever did that is an awful person, and I hope she totally gets busted."

"She? Why 'she'?"

He looked past me to the school. "I just mean whoever. Besides," he continued, "whoever did do it will be sorry if you find out. You really busted out the brute squad."

"What do you mean?"

"I've never seen you so mad. Even I was afraid to say anything to you."

"Really? Huh." I guess I'd fooled everyone. Maybe I was learning something about fake confidence. "But, I'm pretty sure I'm still the school's official biggest loser."

He shrugged his shoulders, keeping his eyes on the ground. "You ain't that bad."

The sun was beginning its descent over the maple trees on the other side of the field, and I realized we'd been sitting for a while. I wanted to get going before school let out.

"Well," I said, standing up and dusting off my butt, "I guess I better go." I started walking back toward the school, but stopped after just a few steps. I turned back to Shiner. "You know what?" I said to him. "You're not that bad either."

Are you overly emotional?

The guy you've been crushing on just said your new haircut is "really interesting." How do you react?

a) By faking cramps and going home to cry in bed for the next two days. You knew you looked like a freak!

b) You tell him, "Thank you," and agree that the new style is interesting and unique.

c) By demanding to know exactly what he means by "interesting"? Is he insulting you?!

I pounded across our front yard through crabgrass and sprouting daffodils, and immediately noticed our Texas flag jerking in the wind. It hadn't been hung since Dad left a few months ago. He used to put it up every morning on his way to work and take it down after dark. Sometimes I'd help hold the flag, being extra careful that it didn't touch the ground. Once, when I was little, I let the corner touch the grass, and I was sure we were going to have to burn the whole thing. But Dad had only winked at me and said, "I won't tell if you won't."

I knew no one would be home—Mom was still at the bank, and Elisabeth was running somewhere like she did every day after school. I was looking forward to crawling in my bed, shutting the blinds, pulling the comforter up over my head, and hiding there for the rest of the evening.

I pushed open our ancient oak front door and immediately noticed something was different. For as long as I could remember, that door had always made a ruckus when we opened it. In the months before Dad moved out, Mom had nagged him every week to oil it, but he never got around to it. He always said he would, but then he'd concentrate on other things like the loose brick we always tripped over on the front steps, the starter on the lawnmower, or the latch on Mom's bedroom window. It wasn't like he wasn't fixing anything—in fact, he loved repairing things. It just seemed like he fixed everything *but*. Dad even told Mom where the WD-40 was so she could fix it herself. It became such a big deal that I even offered to do it. Elisabeth called me a brownnoser, but it seemed easy to do. Mom told me not to bother. A couple of days later, Dad was gone, and Mom hadn't mentioned it since.

Even though I never paid attention anymore to the squeak, I knew instinctively that it was there. But when I opened the door that day, the silence of it was louder than the squeak. And that could only mean one thing:

Dad was home.

He hadn't been there since before Christmas; our yard was still covered in traces of brown leaves that weren't raked for the first fall since I could remember.

Mom and Dad never fought in front of us, not once. It was always in their room, door closed. For the longest time I didn't know what was going on. One evening, when they first started going in there a lot, I searched for Mom. I had a whim to bake cookies, and only she knew where the vanilla extract was. I tried the closed bedroom door, but it was locked.

"Where's Mom?" I'd asked Elisabeth.

"Where do you think?" she had responded mindlessly, stretched across the living room floor. The reflection of MTV images danced across her glazed eyes.

"Their bedroom door is locked," I'd said. Then it hit me, and my first thought was, *Gross!* "You mean they're . . ."

"God, Sara. Grow up," Elisabeth had said. "They're fighting. Again."

After that, I noticed how often their bedroom door was closed. At first, it was only once every couple of weeks. Then every week. Several times a week. Then one day, Dad was gone. We never saw him leave, never even saw him packing his things away, not one box. Mom had taken us to visit our aunt and cousins in Cedar Hill, and by the time we got home late that evening, all of Dad's stuff was gone. I didn't even realize right away that he had left for good.

Mom had sat at the kitchen table drinking tea, and I had snuck in their room to look around. It was weird; Dad had chosen this house in particular because the master bedroom faced west. He didn't want the morning sun to disturb Mom's "beauty rest—not that she needs it." When I went in their room I saw that pictures from their dressers were gone—ones of me and Elisabeth, some of Gram, one of the whole family hiking at Big Bend two years ago. I started to realize Dad wasn't just gone on a long hunting trip—he was really gone. There was a blank spot on the wall, and it took me a moment to remember that it was once covered by a picture of Gram on her wedding day. In the bathroom, Dad's side of the dual sinks and mirrors was completely cleared of razors and shaving cream, toothbrush, comb, the pocketknife he kept in the drawer with his wallet and watch, all gone. The toothpaste marks were still in the sink, from brushing his teeth that morning and the days before. I looked at it, thinking, *Once it's washed, it'll never get dirty again.* I stood looking at the cream-colored countertop, imagining Dad standing there, shaving with the old-fashioned shaving cream and brush I bought him as a Christmas gift when I was in fifth grade and that he'd used ever since.

Look, it's not a big deal. Most kids I know don't live with

both their parents. The point is, on the most horrific day of the school year, in the most horrific semester of my life, I came home and the door didn't squeak. With the squeak gone, it felt like part of my family's past had been erased, and I didn't know how to handle that.

"Hello?" I called out.

I dropped my bag in the entry hall and walked through the living room, where the heads of three of Dad's prize bucks still hung on the wall, black glassy eyes staring into vacancy. I don't even remember Dad bringing them home—that's how long they'd been there. I usually didn't even notice them, but with the door now silent, I felt hyper aware of the house. I heard the back door click shut and heavy footsteps on the linoleum floor in the kitchen.

"Hello?" I said again.

"Sara? It's Dad," he called back as I turned the corner into the kitchen. He carried a box marked CAMPING EQUIP, and his cheeks were pink from the warming spring air, making his smile brighter and seem friendlier. "Hey, baby girl," he said, setting the box down and spreading his arms out to me. I stepped into them tentatively, mindful of my little breasts touching his chest.

"Hey, Dad. What are you doing here?"

"Oh," he said, dropping his truck keys onto the counter. "Just getting a few things out of the attic."

"Mom will be mad if she sees you here." I regretted it instantly, even if it was true.

"I know," he said, eyeing me closely. "That's why I came now, when I thought everyone would be out." He scratched at the day-old stubble on his cheek—he actually hated shaving and only did it for Mom. She used to refuse to kiss him until he'd shaved off the prickly hairs. I wondered if he still had the old-fashioned shaving set I gave him or if he had discarded it, no longer needing to bother. "Haven't seen you in a while. How's school?"

I let out one of those quick, sarcastic laughs. As in, *If you only knew.* But I said, "Fine."

"Yeah?"

"Yes, sir," I responded, looking down at my shoes. "It stinks like always."

"Well, come here, sit down. Tell me what's the matter."

"It's nothing, Dad," I said, still standing. "It's just school. Nobody likes it."

"You know, Sara," he said, resting his hand on my shoulder. "I know we don't talk much anymore, and I know we haven't seen much of each other lately, but I'm still here, and you can talk to me about anything you want. No matter what it might be."

"*Dad.*" I was completely not comfortable talking to him about *this* day. Instead, I said, "Does Mom know you're here?"

"You think it's okay if I get a few more of my things out of storage?" He said it kind of like he was questioning me, and it made me feel like absolute dirt. I mean, it seemed weird that he would have to ask permission to do anything, especially to come into the house he had picked out.

"Sorry, Dad," I said. "It's just that, you know how Mom gets when anything unexpected happens."

"I know. But don't worry about your momma. I'll be out of here in a few minutes. Oh, baby girl," he said, ruffling my hair. "Don't you worry too much. Life isn't just school. Only a small part of it. How're your grades?"

I shrugged. "I bombed a math quiz today."

"Yeah?"

"Systems of equations," I confessed. "I'm terrible at them."

"Well," he said, picking up his keys and jiggling them in his palm, "who isn't?" He smiled at me again, and his eyes looked tired but sweet. He had the bluest eyes in our whole family. Elisabeth's were blue too, but not like Dad's. I had always wished I had eyes like his, but I got Mom's brown ones instead. "Something else bothering you?"

He was making me nervous, standing there like he didn't have a thing to worry about. "Mom's gonna be home soon."

"Wait a sec," he said, glancing up at the round brass clock on the wall we got from Tuesday Morning. "Aren't you supposed to be in school?"

"I left early today."

"Oh, you did, did you? What's this all about?" His voice turned stern, his eyes fixed on me.

I sighed. I wanted to tell him—I needed to tell someone—but I had no idea where to begin. "It's a long story."

He nodded his head and looked down at his palm, rubbing his thumb across it. "Tell you what. How about you and me go get some early dinner. Luby's has Salisbury steak tonight. What do you say?"

Dad's old Ford pickup had a sticker of a kid peeing on the Chevy symbol on the back windshield that Mom had despised. I thought it was gross, too, but I also secretly liked the rare moments when Dad was crass. I was also the only one in the family he joked around with or did outdoorsy stuff with—like hanging the flag and even going to the shooting range. Once a year, Dad went hunting in the mountains of Montana or down to Mexico with a couple of his buddies, and he started going to the shooting range every Saturday two months before his trips. He used to take me with him, but for the life of me I can't figure out why I liked it so much. I'm no fan of hunting, and I'd never even want to hold a gun, but there was something about the indoor shooting range that I liked. I loved wearing the big earphones, and Dad always let me hold the button that whizzes the paper torso target back that shows how well you shot. I'd take those home with me, along with a couple of the fat, red shotgun shells. I loved those plastic shells and would sometimes carry them around in my pocket all week until we went again. It made me feel like we had a special thing going that the girls—Mom and Elisabeth—couldn't understand.

Dad and I hadn't been to Luby's in months. It used to be our thing, before he moved to an apartment in Abilene. When he had first left, he'd come around every so often to see Elisabeth and me; it was always when Mom was working late or when she took a day trip to some seminar in the Panhandle. Elisabeth is always running somewhere or at some classmate's house working on some wonderful project. So, Dad and I would go to Luby's, a cafeteria Elisabeth and Mom would never tolerate. Mom said she quit cafeteria lines when she graduated from high school, and Elisabeth simply said the food stunk. Dad and I loved it. The truth is, I'd probably die if anyone important from school saw me going in there, but I'm always the youngest one by about sixty years. Sometimes Dad and I'd talk about stuff—my crappy math grades, a Razzie movie Arlene and I were trying to find—and sometimes we didn't talk about anything. We'd just sit there and eat quietly, and the ladies who filled up our iced tea glasses always smiled brightly at Dad and asked him how he was doing and such. I think they were flirting with him, which made me uncomfortable and proud at the same time.

"So," Dad started as he took a long gulp from his tea—he liked it extra sugary. "How's Arlene? You two up to no good?"

I hesitated before shoving a forkful of mashed potatoes with cream gravy in my mouth. "We're up to no nothing." Which I knew didn't make any sense, but I didn't know what to tell him.

"Well," he said. "You get busier the older you get."

"I'm not busy."

"Well. Come out with it, then."

"It's long and complicated," I said wearily. "And I don't have the energy."

"Sometimes it's better to just be out with it." He cut his Salisbury steak, then laid his knife across the top of his plate.

"Anyway. I'd have no idea where to start."

Dad chewed thoughtfully. "Arlene do something to rile you up?"

I sighed. "Yes, sir. Not to mention the rest of the school." I pushed my food around on my plate. "Dad? Back when you were in high school, were there popular kids who were nauseatingly perfect?"

"I suspect there've been popular kids since the beginning of the schoolhouse," he said, looking off toward the dessert cart. "They're nothing new. Is that what's been bothering you? A bunch of popular kids?"

"A little. I don't know." We sat for a moment. And then I

said, "It just seems like they've got it so easy. And it seems like popular people can only breed popular kids. Plus, they're always gorgeous, athletic, and smart, too. It's like they're all a part of this system that'll never let outsiders in. These people, Dad, they have everything." I realized I had started to raise my voice there at the end a little bit, but when I looked around, no one seemed to have noticed. Dad nodded his head slowly. "I know it's totally generic to be jealous of them, but it's not fair. What's wrong with wanting to be like them?"

"Nothing, I suppose."

"Exactly. I mean, in all the stupid magazines they're always telling us to be ourselves, to not care what people think, to love the body we have and all that."

Dad looked up at me, his mouth tight.

"Sorry," I said. "It's just that they tell us to be ourselves, but who wouldn't want to look like the girls in those same magazines, wearing cool clothes and having perfect hair all the time? And like actresses, too. Did you see the Academy Awards?" I asked, knowing full well he didn't. "They are all so perfect, and I know they're all prettied up for the event, but still. You can't deny they're gorgeous." Okay, even I could tell I might be on a whining track now, but sometimes with Dad, it's easy to get going. He says so little that he makes me want to fill the silence.

"Yep," he said, leaning back in his chair and loosening

his belt one notch. "Yep, I guess I know what you mean. I remember when I was in high school, a little bit older than you, there was this one fella who was real popular. The girls were always slipping anonymous notes in his locker, and people seemed to like him just because he was good in sports. Then he got voted Valentine King at the dance, and he didn't show. He probably figured the kids would think he was an arrogant jerk if he didn't show, but they didn't. Seemed to make them like him more."

"See what I mean? They get away with everything."

"Well," he said, "the thing is, not everyone wants that. When you're popular, people think they have you pegged. And that's not very fair. There's more to people than what they look like. Sometimes they could have a hundred friends but feel like they've got no one to confide in. Things aren't always what they seem. Don't you forget that."

"I guess," I said, considering that. "I just feel like everyone is watching me when I don't want them to, and no one is looking when I do. That sounds dumb, I guess." I took a last scoop of potatoes, then dropped my fork on the plate with a decisive *plunk*.

"Oh, honey," he said, pushing his finished plate forward and leaning his elbows on the table. Mom hated it when we did that, even if we were finished eating. "No one is watching you."

"Humph," was all I managed.

The dessert cart lady came rolling up to our table. "Y'all want something here?" She was old and looked way past retirement, and I wondered if she had to work at Luby's or if she just liked being there. I wondered if, back when she was in high school, fifty years ago, she could have ever guessed that this would be her life. Was she disappointed now, or happy?

"Want some pecan pie, baby?" Dad asked.

I rubbed my hand across my belly. "No thanks. I'm full," I said, even though pecan is my all-time favorite. I'd worked myself up so much that my stomach was in knots.

"No, thank you," Dad said to the lady. She smiled and rolled away. "We better get you home before your momma sends out an Amber Alert on you."

He reached over and patted me twice on my thigh—I could feel it jiggle even as I tried to flex it—and smiled at me.

As we drove back past Jefferson Ford, I thought of what I might become if only I could de-geekify myself. I asked Dad, "So whatever happened to the Valentine King? He marry some hottie and grow up to be rich and enormously happy?"

Dad smiled, his wrist resting on the steering wheel, gently guiding the car. "He did marry a hottie, yes. Grew up to be pretty dern happy. In high school, grown up is a long ways off, it seems. When it catches up with you, you know that those silly awards in school meant nothing." He cocked his head and asked, "Do I still look like a Valentine King to you?"

My dad. Who'd've thunk it? I could never imagine him as the catch of the county or whatever he was called back in the day, but he was certainly sweet enough. He hadn't grown up rich at all, either. Gram and Gramps still had chickens and pigs and stuff when Dad was growing up, he'd once told me. It sort of shot my theory of the breeding aspect of things.

When we pulled into the driveway, Mom's car was there, and Elisabeth's bedroom light was on. My belly was full, and my mind was feeling happy and relaxed again. Time with Dad always did that to me.

"Before you go inside, there's something I want to give you," he said, reaching over to the glove compartment. He held his fist over my hand and said, "Well, here you go." I opened my hand and in plopped a dusty red shotgun shell. "Remember how you used to love picking these things up? I grabbed one the other day, thought you might like to hold on to it again."

I squeezed the empty shell in my hand, feeling the ridges along the sides. In that moment, I think I knew that my dad was sad about the past. Not his high school past, but maybe the time with my mom. Holding the shell in my hand, I realized that things had been pretty easy. And I knew, without realizing, that from here on out, nothing would ever be that easy again.

♥10♥

Are Your Parents Totally Unfair or Are You Totally Unreasonable?

Just as you're heading out the door to meet Mara and Eileen at the movies, your mother stops you and says you have to do the dishes before you leave. How do you react?

a) By refusing to do them until you get home—even if it means groundation

b) By asking your mother if you could please do them as soon as you get home

c) By doing them right away, even though that means missing the previews—your favorite part of any movie

When I said nothing would be easy, I didn't mean that things would get worse before Dad could even back out of the driveway. As I walked through the squeak-less door, I saw Mom, standing front and center in her boxy blue suit and navy pumps, fists on hips.

"Young lady, just where have you been?"

I rubbed my thumb over the red shell squeezed tight in my fist. "Dad was here. He took me to Luby's."

"In this house," she began through gritted teeth, "we ask permission before we go somewhere. Next time your father takes you out, you either call me or leave me a note. Understand?"

"Yes, ma'am."

She stepped closer to me, hands still propped up on her hips like she was about to order me to drop and give her twenty. "Anything else you want to tell me about?"

I held on to the dim hope that she didn't know about my leaving school early without permission. "No, ma'am."

Mom clenched her jaw before saying, "I'm going to ask you one more time. Is there anything else you want to tell me about?"

I knew this tactic, but in the moment, I was too panicked. Mom hated lying more than back-talking or yelling. Still, I clung to desperate hope—it felt like that was all I had left. So I shook my head and said, "No, ma'am."

She rolled her lips in on each other and sucked in air through her nose, nodding her head knowingly. "Two weeks," she announced, propping two fingers up in a gesture that definitely didn't mean "peace." "One class equals one week. And for the lying, that'll get you another."

Apparently the school keeps careful track of these things

and had called Mom as soon as they got word I wasn't there. I could just hear Mrs. Nicholson saying to Mom, "We just wanted to make sure everything was *okay*." Like she was doing me a personal favor.

"But Mom, next week is spring break. You already said I could go skiing with Kirstie!"

"Lower your voice," she snapped. "You should have thought about that just now when you told me a bold-faced lie *and* decided to take an early dismissal from school. Do I look stupid to you?"

"But they're expecting me," I cried. She couldn't take this away from me—especially after what had been done to my locker, it was the only thing keeping me from going completely over the edge. I was the biggest laughingstock of Bowie Junior High—I needed this trip to make people see me as a sophisticated traveler with stories that would help erase what had happened that day.

"Listen to me, young lady. You've had a poor attitude for weeks now. Now I'm sorry about the ski trip, but allowing you to go at this point is like rewarding you for your bad behavior." Mom took a deep breath and slowly released it. "Sara, honey, I don't know what's going on with you lately, but whatever it is I want you to know you can talk to me about it—"

"I want to go to Aspen!"

"Forget it," she said with a sweep of her hands. "Until you can stop acting like a brat, we're not discussing this any further."

Unspeakably pissed, I turned on my heel and headed to the tiny comfort of my room. As I slammed my bedroom door shut, the framed picture of me and Arlene on the Judge Roy Bean ride at Six Flags rattled on the wall. I folded my arms across my chest, tears welling up in my eyes as I stared at the photo. I stuck my tongue out, then flipped it off. I knew it was childish, but I didn't care. Thanks to Arlene, my life was an official nightmare.

I wiped my face, picked up my phone, and dialed.

"Hey," I said when Kirstie answered her phone. "It's Sara."

"Hey, girl. What's up? I was just about to call you."

"Yeah? Well, I've got some bad news." I could hear a TV in the background, something with laughing and music. I swallowed before going on. "I skipped last period, and my mom found out. She totally freaked and grounded me for the entire spring break. Aspen is out."

"Oh, my God, please don't tell me this!" Kirstie said. "I was going to call you and tell you that Jason is going to be there too. The same hotel and everything."

"Are you kidding me?" I lurched to the edge of my bed. Talk about the opportunity of a lifetime—the chance to be alone with Jason, in another state no less, surrounded by fresh air and mountains, snowflakes dusting my cheeks that could be easily kissed away. Prime Jason time gone, like a cold snap of the Rocky Mountain wind.

"I feel horrible," Kirstie said. "He told me when he walked me to my class after your locker. I wanted to do a little fact-finding to help you with your Class Favorite thing, so I started chatting and we ended up talking about spring break and what we were doing . . . oh, Sara. This is awful! And after the day you had."

"Tell me about it," I said. I thought that once you hit rock bottom, things could only get better. I'd been hitting a new rock bottom for weeks now.

"I'm coming!" Kirstie hollered away from the phone. "Listen, I gotta get going. Mom's taking me shopping for some new snowboarding pants. Oh," she said. "Am I so insensitive for telling you that? Should I have not said anything?"

"No, it's fine," I told her, even though knowing about it only made me feel worse.

After I hung up the phone, I tried to convince myself that *this* was my final rock bottom. I couldn't get any lower than this. Right?

With less than two months to go until people were nominated for Class Favorite (it happened a few weeks before the end of school so they could get the pictures in the yearbook), I realized I hadn't been taking my mission of stepping out of loserville and into Class Favorite-ville seriously enough. I was tired of being laughed at, making a fool of myself and being a general freak at Bowie Junior High, so this is what I did:

First, I wallowed. I wallowed, and then I fumed. Life was not fair. I had been a good person up to this point in my life. I never cheated on tests, and I never stole so much as a piece of Brach's candy from the grocery store. I didn't smoke or drink. I once called the city of Ladel to get them to come scrape a cat off the road, not because it grossed me out but because I didn't want some kid to drive by with his parents and see his once-Fluffy turned to a pancake. I thought of others. I tried to be good. And now, this is where it'd gotten me: stuck home during spring break while Jason, The Boy Who Could Have Been, went skiing without me, the girl who might have been his Only. If I had been able to go to Aspen, not only would Jason have become smitten with me, but when we came back to school, me on his arm like Hollywood royalty, I could definitely have been in the running for a Class Favorite nomination. I mean, who else could go from feminine products–covered locker to Girlfriend of a God in two weeks flat? For now, there was just one person standing in my way of my dreams becoming reality: Mom. She was the last person I wanted to talk to at that moment, considering she was responsible for keeping me from my goals. Rage had me in its tight clutches, our fight and my grounding still fresh, open wounds. But this was the biggest battle of my life, and I had to suck down any pride I had left and go begging.

Beg doesn't seem sufficient enough a word to describe how I asked Mom if I could go to Aspen, despite being grounded. I pleaded with her. I even beseeched and implored. I'm talking on-my-knees, hands-clasped-to-my-chest, weepy-eyes pleading—the kind of begging that Mary did for Jesus. It was a Nicole Kidman kind of performance—a thing of beauty.

I followed her into the kitchen and watched her drag a chair to the center of the linoleum, right beneath the frosted glass–covered light. "Mom, listen. *Please*. You can ground me for two whole months when I get back. I'll do anything. I'll cook dinner for a month. I'll do the dishes for two!"

"Sara, honey, I'm sorry. But when I say no, I mean no." She did look sympathetic as she stepped up on the chair and unscrewed the cover, then stepped down to put the light cover on the counter. "I certainly don't condone truancy, and you know how I feel about lying. That's just something I can't stand for. No, sir." She screwed in the new lightbulb and looked happily at the fresh, bright light.

Couldn't she understand how important this was? Didn't she have friends, a *life* when she was my age? To make things worse, I had this nagging worry that Kirstie and Jason would hook up in Aspen. It's possible I was just being paranoid, but I thought about how she had pulled him away from me after the locker incident. If they came back as a couple, I'd die—probably just after watching them being nominated eighth-grade Class Favorites. I couldn't let that happen. Losing the trip to Aspen felt like losing all hope.

I decided to tell my mom about my locker not just as a way to score some sympathy, but because I wanted her to know that there were real reasons for the way I'd been acting. "Things have been pretty bad at school lately. Arlene and I aren't talking. And then . . . well, someone did something to my locker. Someone put a bunch of . . . female stuff on it."

"Did you tell the principal?"

I looked at her as she walked to the sink to wash her hands. She looked over her shoulder at me, waiting. "Mom, are you listening? I said someone put some things on my locker. Some *woman* things."

"Sara, if something's going on at school, you should talk to your principal about it. Defacing school property is a crime." She dried her hands on a clean towel, then dropped it on the counter. I couldn't believe she didn't get anything I'd been saying. Just a month ago she was paying too much attention to me—now she wasn't even listening.

"Mom, someone put a bunch of *tampons* on my locker— the *outside* of my locker." Suddenly I didn't have to try to force the tears—they came freely and fast. "And the whole school saw it. Do you know why someone did this to my locker? Because everyone knows about the period roses that *you* humiliated me with. The worst part is my own best friend did it to me. Now the only person who will talk to me is Kirstie, and you won't let me do even that. I just want to get out of here—can't you understand?"

I turned on my heel and ran to my room, but careful not to slam my door—God forbid she tacks on another two weeks of groundation.

I did a belly flop onto my bed, buried my face in my pillow, and cried. Mom came to my door and knocked softly, gently calling my name. I didn't answer, and she left me alone. I could tell by the tone of her voice she was sorry, but I didn't care—she *should* feel bad.

I knew crying wasn't going to get me anywhere. If I wanted to make changes in my life, I would have to make them myself— I couldn't rely on Kirstie to take me to Aspen or on my mom to let me go. Sitting around and waiting for my name to magically appear on the Class Favorite ballot wouldn't work. It was all on my shoulders, and I had to figure a way to make things right. After too much time wasted, I got down to work.

With the theme music to *Rocky* playing in my head, I sprang out of bed and gathered up all my magazines, old and new, even the ones under my bed from almost a year ago. I got my Class Favorite Qualities list out of my messenger bag and smoothed it on my desk. I pulled my yearbooks from the last two years off my bookshelf. I opened up my spiral notebook, the magazines and yearbooks, and spread them all before me on the carpet.

I got a pair of scissors and some blank paper, and started flipping through the magazines. I cut out articles like "Love

Your Beautiful Self . . . Now!" for advice on confidence and ones titled "Find Your Foxy Physique in Five Fast Fitness Fixes" for help on my outward appearance. Then I went to the back of the magazines, where I knew all the fashion pages were, and cut out looks and outfits I thought I needed. I cut out pictures of Haden Prescott from the tabloids and taped them to my wall. I had one picture of her at the Oscars, and another shot of her from *Demon's Lover*. I pasted them side-by-side to keep reminding myself that anything was possible.

In addition to all the qualities on the Class Favorite list I had made with Kirstie, I knew there was one thing I needed to accomplish: I had to get them to come to me. I could talk to all the popular people I wanted—and I intended to approach them often—but they'd never see me as worthy until they actually liked me. Once they started talking to me in the halls, calling me on the phone and inviting me to their parties, I'd know I'd made it. So, I decided I needed to concentrate on three things: I had to look good, act confident, and be more social. These were the basics of any nominee, I realized—both Academy Award and Class Favorite. You had to put yourself out there and make people notice you. You had to charm them. And I intended to do just that.

Next, while Mom was at the grocery store, I took my yearbooks to Jim's Grocery, a small convenience store near our house, and made copies of pages with former Class Favorite nominees and winners, then pasted their pictures above my desk. I wrote below them certain vitals:

ROSEMARY VICKERS

<u>HAIR</u>: THICK; <u>MAKEUP</u>: MINIMAL; <u>CLOTHES</u>: CHIC;

<u>DEMEANOR</u>: COMPOSED

<u>DATING HISTORY</u>: ERIC GREENE (ABOUT 4 MONTHS),

JEREMY DAHL (TWO MONTHS?)

<u>NICE?</u>: ALWAYS!

<u>FRIENDS</u>: TONS! WHO DOESN'T LIKE HER?!

<u>HOTNESS</u>: 9.5

<u>X FACTOR</u>: SHE'S UNDERSTATED? (ACK!)

Then, after pasting pictures of great outfits from magazines onto blank pages and taping them next to the CF photos, I went to my closet and dumped just about everything onto my bed, shoes onto the floor. I picked through salvageable items, and put the rest into a huge Goodwill pile.

I stood back and looked at the mess I had made, then I inspected myself in the mirror: my hair (straight, thin, dirt brown, and a boring, nonexistent cut); my clothes (jeans with a denim shirt—could I be any more generic?); my body (okay for now, but was my belly starting to stick out too much?). I shook my head at my reflection, disappointed. I thought about the kinds of girls who could get boyfriends in a heartbeat: Rosemary, with her thick, wavy hair the color of exotic fruit; Kayla, her perfect little body and so-confident attitude. I looked at the Class Favorite pictures and stats I had made: grades, beauty, friends. Glancing at myself in the mirror again, I noticed that my arms looked a little flabby. I quickly knelt down to the floor and did eight pushups, the most I could do. I stood up, looked at my reflection again, and sighed.

I had a long way to go.

♥ 11 ♥

Find Your Inner Flirt

You're finally ready to—subtly—let Lucas know you think he's totally hot. While you're both in the lunch line, you:

a) wink at him, smile, and walk away.

b) briefly make eye contact before grabbing a Snapple and bolting to your table.

c) get behind him in line, tell him you like his jeans, and ask him, with a hint of coy, why the two of you haven't hooked up yet.

I stepped through the front doors of Bowie on the first day after spring break feeling nervous but excited. My hope was that the entire school had forgotten about the incident with my locker, and the flowers. Surely they'd created better memories in Cancún or wherever. So I didn't have great travel tales to dazzle everyone with. I had done something more important over the break: I had laid out my war plan, and now I intended to execute it.

I was finally taking my goal of getting on the Class Favorite ballot seriously. It was the only way to rise above the misery that had become my life—Sara, Plain and Hysterical—and I had just over a month to do it. Also, with Arlene out of my life and Kirstie out of state, I'd been really lonely, so working on my plan at least gave me something to do. The only person to talk to was Mom, who had tried her best to make the grounding up to me after Elisabeth told her just how bad the locker incident had been (I had confessed it all to Elisabeth late one night). Mom said she had thought I was overreacting just to get her to let me go skiing. When she found out the truth, she felt terrible and even made cupcakes with pink icing like when I was five years old. They tasted unusually good, maybe because period number two of the Life of Sara Thurman was creeping up. Welcome to my spring break.

Other than indulging in the occasional sweet treat, I obsessed over my goal of becoming a Class Favorite by telling myself I was a confident, mature woman who could win any award I put my mind to. And if that didn't work, I also came up with looks and outfits to show people like Jason how spectacularly . . . er . . . spectacular I was on the outside. Still, it wasn't the only thing I thought about. There was the little fact that Arlene and I hadn't spoken for weeks now.

I sort of missed her. Okay, I *really* missed her, even if I was furious with her. Why, why, why did she have to do this to me? Had her softball friends convinced her I was a loser hanger-on, and that was her way of getting rid of me? Couldn't she have come up with something a little less ... public, if that was the case?

On the first day back, I wore one of the new outfits I had begged Mom to buy me. I made my case for new clothes by (only slightly!) fibbing that I had outgrown a lot of my stuff. She finally gave me a small allowance, but insisted on giving Elisabeth the same amount of money *and* made her go shopping with me. Elisabeth only gave me a smirk as a sign of her appreciation.

Of course, it wasn't much money—we're not rich—so Elisabeth and I had decided to go to Clothestime since they're cheap and were having a sale.

"You better swear not to tell anyone we came here," Elisabeth had said as she cut the engine on Mom's Civic. "This is just as bad as being caught at Kmart."

"Please. You're not the only one with a reputation, you know," I had said.

I wore a red-and-black plaid skirt that came farther above my knee than the school dress code allowed and a cap-sleeve top that was tighter than my mom would allow. When I left the house that morning, I wore my new yellow button-up sweater over the tight top; once I got to school I tied it around my waist. I also had on a pair of knee-high fake leather boots, just like the ones Rosemary Vickers had (except hers were probably real leather). The only thing that wasn't perfect was the red Rudolph Christmas socks complete with plastic eyes I had to wear since the laundry needed to be done, but they were safely tucked into my boots. The whole outfit made me look smart, but hot. I was sure of it—Haden Prescott would highly approve.

I felt great walking through the halls, full of confidence. It was like everyone was looking at me differently, I could just feel it. I walked regally, with my head high, barely noticing people as I passed. I wanted to be elusive, just like in an article titled "Six Sly Ways to Push His Hot Buttons" I read in *Cosmo*.

Things started off well—Coach Eckels caught up with me in the halls before I even hit first period.

"Thurman!" he hollered as I closed my locker and started toward English. "Come here a second. I want to talk to you."

At first I thought, *Great. What'd I do now?* Was it my too-mini skirt?

"Yes, sir?"

"Listen, I'm in a bind and need some help. What are you doing after school today?"

"Nothing, I guess. I mean," I quickly added, thinking of my scholarly Class Favorite qualities, "probably some homework."

"The boys got a basketball game after school against Sam Houston. I need someone to take stats for the game. There's only a couple more games left in the season, but we'll need someone for those, too. I'd need you there for the warm-up before the game and to help put equipment away afterward. You'd be in charge of keeping all the stats for the boys so we know who does good and who's not pulling his weight. You interested?"

I couldn't believe it. Had my sister finally pulled through a favor for me? And it was all happening on the day I was wearing my best new outfit. As a stat girl in this outfit, people—especially Jason—were going to notice me.

Then someone came up behind me and knocked the backs of my knees, making me almost crumple to the ground right there in front of Coach Eckels. Before I could turn and see who it was, Coach bellowed, "Camry! What in the hell are you doing?"

When I turned around, I saw a clearly mortified Shiner frozen in his imitation-Timberland boots.

"Apologize to this lady right now," Coach demanded, with a stiff finger pointed at me.

"Oh . . . uh, sorry, Thurman," he said, looking down at the floor.

"Camry, I swear," Coach muttered. "Get on to class, now, boy." Coach Eckels sighed, shaking his head. Then he turned back to me. "So, you want the job?"

"Yeah, sure. Yes, sir," I corrected. "What time you want me to be there?"

Normally I would have run and told Arlene first thing. Instead, I did my best not to get too down about her, because after talking to Coach Eckels, I felt great. Not only would I get closer to Jason, but it just seemed like heaven—being around all the guys, sitting on the bench, flirting with them in my knee-high boots. This was going to be a huge turning point for me. I mean, this was paradise.

When I sat down in my cold chair in English class, my skirt barely covered my butt, and my legs stuck to the seat. I kept tugging at the end of the skirt to try to pull it down, but it didn't do much good. I kept my knees locked together and I concentrated on how hot and aloof I looked.

I must have truly looked good because as Jason settled into his seat, he stretched across the aisle to tap his pen on my desk.

"Hey," he said. "I like those boots."

I smiled, trying to stay calm, but I was about to burst. "Thanks. So do you."

He laughed and sat back in his seat while I cringed.

Everyone was talking and bouncing around the room, still wound up from spring break. Ms. Galarza was shuffling papers at her desk and didn't seem to notice or mind.

"So how was your break?" Jason asked, turning back to me.

Coincidence that Jason was talking to me on that particular day? Doubtful.

But I played it cool by rolling my eyes and shaking my head. "Horrible. I was supposed to go skiing with Kirstie in Aspen. Did you see her there?"

"Yeah," he said. "We did a couple of runs together."

"Oh," I said. *Aloof, aloof,* I told myself as I tried not to decipher the tone of his voice. "Sounds cool."

"It was all right," he said.

My stomach did a quick flip-flop. All right? That did *not* sound like smitten mile-high love to me.

"She kicked my butt on the double diamonds. She's a machine on that snowboard."

"Oh," I said, stomach sinking. Butt kicking didn't sound like love, I thought, but it could be bonding—which might be worse.

As Ms. Galarza settled us in, I braved a glance at Arlene. Her skin was just as pale as mine; I wondered if she had stayed home too. I watched as she sat back in her chair, and when she looked around the room, our eyes locked for a moment. I was the first to look away, but moments later, I could still feel her eyes on me.

Later that day, as I spun the combination of my locker, a hip bumped into mine.

"You look cute," Kirstie said, looking down at my outfit.

I smoothed my skirt down over my hips. "Thanks," I said. "So, come on, tell me. How was Colorado?"

"Pretty amazing, actually. Perfect powder every day, kinda warm, sunny skies. Couldn't have asked for better conditions.

Actually"—she dug in her bag and pulled out a plastic bag—"I got this for you." I opened the bag and found a T-shirt, a scented candle, and a key chain. "The candle supposedly smells like an aspen leaf. And the key chain is also one of those leaves. It's pewter."

"Oh, thanks," I said, surprised. "You didn't have to do that."

"I felt bad about the whole not-being-able-to-go thing. It would have been so much better with you."

I put the loot in my locker before we headed toward science. "Jason said y'all hung out some."

"We did a couple of runs together. That was all."

"Oh," I said. I wondered if she was holding something back—maybe they both were. I tried to shake my mind of these negative thoughts as we entered our science class and Ms. Cowell was already yelling at us.

"Okay, everyone," Ms. Cowell called from the front of the room. Even her cheeks looked a little rosier than usual, and I wondered where she had gone. Being a teacher and all, she probably went someplace weird like the Houston Museum of Natural History. "We've got finals coming up in just a few weeks and a lot of work to do."

"Hey, Thurman," Shiner whispered from across the row. He had his dirty white Cowboys baseball hat on backward, and his skin looked worse than usual. He was red-burned looking. "Hey, you seen Mrs. Everly yet?"

I shook my head. "No. Why?"

"Jimmy, please take that hat off in my classroom," Ms. Cowell told him.

He took it off and turned toward the front of the room, his thin hair mushed on his head. The room was frigid, so I took my yellow sweater from my book bag and slipped my arms through it. Even though this was not my original vision of hotness for the first day back, I was sure I still looked smokin'.

"Turn to chapter twelve, please," Ms. Cowell said.

I pulled my book from my bag and looked back over at Shiner. He leaned down by the side of his desk to get his book and looked at my skirt as I tugged it down toward my knees. I glared at him, wondering if he was trying to get a look up the skirt. He leaned a little across the aisle toward me and whispered, "Your outfit."

He was trying to tell me what I already knew—that the skirt was too short. But I didn't care. It was fifth period and I hadn't gotten in trouble for it yet—I knew I was in the clear, and soon I'd be on that basketball court, making the guys wonder what took them so long to notice my hotness.

But when I walked into algebra and took one look at Mrs. Everly, I realized that Shiner was only trying to save me from yet another humiliation.

♥**12**♥

What Your Spring Style Says About You

On the first warm day of spring, you're most likely to be seen wearing:

a) the same black clothes you wore during winter, except maybe your shirt is short sleeved instead of long sleeved

b) jeans, sneakers, and a comfortable tee—something that will allow you to pop into an impromptu soccer game if need be

c) the most adorable spaghetti-strapped sundress, even though it's still a little chilly out

Like I said before, Mrs. Everly is an old lady. I don't say that to be mean but to hammer home a crucial point. She's at least, I don't know, fifty or sixty. Whatever, she has gray hair, and the skin on her neck sort of wobbles when she talks, and her entire body is what the magazines call "pear shaped," which is just a nice way of saying all-over fat.

The funny part was, the first thing I saw when I walked into her algebra class was Shiner. He was looking right at me, like he'd been eagerly waiting for me, this concerned expression on his face that was totally unfamiliar to me. He was sitting real straight, his leg jiggling like crazy, tapping his pencil on his desk. He looked like he'd downed a whole keg of Coke for lunch.

Three seconds later, I realized what Shiner had been talking about when he whispered, "Your outfit."

Mrs. Everly stood at the board with her back to us wearing—what else?—a red-and-black plaid skirt, a yellow sweater, and—you guessed it—black leather boots. Her skirt was longer, she wore black pantyhose, her sweater was quite baggy, and her boots were not shiny pleather, but there she stood before me and the entire class, wearing the exact same outfit as me.

I froze before I could make it to my seat. That's when I heard the snickering. It was a couple of jerks on the other side of the room. I couldn't see them, but I could hear them.

"Wait till I tell Jessica," Kayla said to Sean.

I clutched my books to my chest, trying to cover up as much of my outfit as possible—totally *im*possible. I slinked to my desk and immediately slumped down in my chair, but my thighs squeaked in protest on the way down, pinching me to a halt. I stretched the sweater as tightly across my body as I could.

Truth be told, when I nervously looked around the room,

not everyone was staring at me, laughing their worry-free heads off. Rosemary was looking through her notebook, and Jason was writing something on a scrap of paper. But Kayla and Sean—who was now laughing—were enough. Then I caught Shiner's eye.

"I tried to tell you," he whispered from across the rows, his brows raised in concern.

Mrs. Everly went over some new systems of equations thing since the exam was coming up. To make sure we all understood how to do it, she had us go up to the board in groups of three and work out a problem. I was in the third group with Shiner and Rosemary, who gave me a pity smile as she looked down at my itchy skirt.

There I stood, exposed in front of the entire class. Then Mrs. Everly said, "You have nice taste in clothing, Sara," like she was the most clever person on earth. "Isn't Clothestime just wonderful?"

A few people tried to stifle their laughter while Rosemary and Shiner hurriedly worked on their problems. I glared back at her and her old wrinkly face. She pricked up her brows and said, "Though I must say that skirt looks a bit short for the school dress code."

I tugged on the coarse, ugly thing, once again wishing it would give just a little, wishing I could drown out the laughter that Mrs. Everly was ignoring. Teachers never enforced the no-talking-in-class rule when you needed them to. She just let them run wild, at my expense.

I glanced back at Jason. He was just looking at me. Not laughing, not looking with pity . . . just looking. It made me sad for him, thinking he might be sad for me—or maybe embarrassed for me. I realized that becoming a Class Favorite nominee might not be as easy as I had hoped, so I told myself to act confident, even if I felt like a total loser. So I flashed him a smile while rolling my eyes, pretending I didn't care even though the chalk in my hand felt cold and dry and I thought I might start bawling.

"I think it looks good on you," Rosemary whispered as she hurried back to her seat, snapping me back to attention.

My Class Favorite heroine, Rosemary Vickers, knew just what to say, even to a lowlife like me. The gratification I felt was like being saved from hungry tigers in the Colosseum. I wrestled with my problem on the board—got it wrong, natch—went back to my desk and silently begged for a nuclear explosion while trying to keep a nonchalant expression on my face. I had a feeling, though, that I looked more constipated than carefree.

I bolted out the door when the bell rang, wondering how many people in the entire school had Mrs. Everly for a teacher. Using my brilliant math skills (academics, No. 6 on the list), I figured there were twenty-five people per class, seven classes per day . . . 175. Nice. That was like a fourth of the school. And I still had to go do stats for the basketball game, now a blessing and a curse. I'd have to stay in the getup and hope Mrs. Everly didn't go to the game, but at least I got to be with the basketball boys . . . and Jason. The silver lining in the thunderstorm of my life.

"Hey, Thurman!"

I turned around in the hall at the sound of a guy's voice. Jason's voice.

"Wait up," he called.

Oh, my God. *He* was approaching *me*. My Class Favorite goal was actually falling into place. But what could he want? To offer me pity? To tell me it's time to consider vocational education, where clothes aren't as revered? My Rudolph socks were slipping toward my ankles, causing my pleather-clad calves to sweat. My armpits were sweating too. I was a mess.

"Hey," I said coolly. "What's up?"

"Listen," he said as we walked down the crowded hall together. "Can I ask you a question?"

"Yes?" I think I actually batted my eyelashes as I anticipated answering what could potentially be the most important question of my life.

He smiled this wicked sweet smile that was all soap-opera charm. Then he asked, "How do you keep getting yourself into these situations?"

I could feel my plastered, trying-to-be-casual smile pull down my face. "Huh?"

"You're always . . ." He paused, raising his hands in a loss for words. "I don't know. Just . . . getting yourself into these weird situations. Like your outfit today. Or your locker. Which sucked, I know. But the way you handle everything. You seem like you stay so sane through it all. That's pretty cool."

He wasn't making fun of me. I could hear the sincerity in his voice. We continued down the hall together, slowly. Out in the open. For anyone in all of Bowie Junior High to see. I wondered where the yearbook photographer was when you needed her.

"Thanks," I answered, wishing he hadn't brought up—or even remembered—the locker incident. I started to wonder if all that confidence and poise from my Class Favorite list that I'd been trying to exude even before spring break had actually come through. "But I'm pretty sure it's all just a facade."

He laughed. "Well, this is my class." We stopped in front of Mr. Rickles's room. "I'll see ya later, Sara." He turned to walk inside his class.

Sara. He called me Sara, not Thurman. In the space of a single junior high hallway, I had gone from classmate Thurman to girl Sara. He said my name like a breath—*Saaara*. Totally swoon-worthy.

" 'Kay," I croaked. "Later." But as I turned to go, I had a moment of bravery. "Oh, hey, Jason?"

He stepped back outside the door, tossing his bangs out of his amber eyes.

"What's up?" he asked.

"If you ever find yourself without something cool to wear, just call me. I know where Coach Eckels shops."

He smiled. "I'll keep that in mind."

"Cool," I said, all casual. "But don't tell anyone, 'kay?"

He nodded and said, "Secret's safe." He turned back toward his class and, looking over his shoulder at me, said, "See you later, Sara."

♥ 13 ♥

Can You Tell a Friend from a Foe?

You lost a note from your friend, Casey, that had some very private information on it regarding her—*gulp!*—"feminine freshness" problem. To make matters worse, most of the football team found out. She said she forgives you; now, you need to confide in her about the problems your parents are having. Is there a chance she'll turn on you, just to get even?

a) Slight chance—I'd be leery of telling her anything too big, too soon.

b) No chance, no way, no how.

c) Big chance—I can't ever tell her another secret as long as I live.

I was flying. After talking to Jason, I knew that nothing could get me down. Even though my life of late had become a series of ups and downs more stomach-dropping than the Superman Tower of Power ride, I felt that talking to Jason gave me the boost I needed to sail through the rest of the year—or the rest of the day, at least. When Coach Eckels had asked me that morning to do the stats, I had wanted to jump right out of my pleather boots. But after the humiliation in Mrs. Everly's class, I was feeling a bit gun-shy. I wanted to talk to *someone* before stepping into the boys' basketball stat world. I longed for encouragement from Arlene or attitude advice from Kirstie. I would have settled for a nice word from Dad.

I hadn't heard from him since he took me to dinner at Luby's. I'd e-mailed him twice over spring break and called his office once but hadn't heard back. I figured he must be back on the road, and there would be a postcard from Louisiana or Oklahoma waiting for me at home.

I called Mom at work to let her know I'd be home late. She cheered me on, as if I'd actually made the team, but somehow it made me feel good. I headed to the gym, where the boys were warming up, shooting baskets from the free-throw line before doing some layup drills. The stands were filling up with parents and students. A bunch of Sam Houston Rebels were stretching and shooting easy baskets at the other end of the court.

All the best guys were on the team, and so was Shiner. I stood for a moment inside the gym doors, watching them— the irregular *pat-pat-pat* of basketballs hitting the gym floor, echoing with each dribble; the squeaking of shoes on the shiny hardwood court. Guys shuffled around at each end, arms outstretched, waiting for the ball to be passed to them. I felt a rush just watching them.

Jason was dribbling the ball low to the court. He did a fake right, then went left around Richie Adams before the ball *tip . . . tip . . . tipped* into the basket. As the ball fell through the net, he casually walked away, wiping his forehead with the palm of his hand, then wiping his hand on his baggy shorts.

"Over here!" Shiner yelled. He was wide open, but no one passed the ball to him. He just stood to the left of the court, his hand held over his head like you'd ask a question in class. "Adams! Come on, I'm open!"

Richie ignored him from the half-court line, looking for someone else to pass to. But then Shiner skated across the court, effortlessly stole the ball from Richie, did a spin-turn around Frankie Donnelly, and went in for an easy layup. The ball bounced listlessly when it came down, and Shiner turned to pick it back up.

"I told you I was open," he said to Richie, and then chucked the ball at him.

I cracked a smile—that was the Shiner I remembered from when we were kids. He didn't like being ignored, especially when he knew he was right.

The stands were filling up with gawking girls and supportive parents. Kayla Cane sat in the stands at the end of the court where our guys were warming up. She wore a short denim skirt and flip-flopping heels, and her dark brown hair fell in soft curls over her tanned shoulders. Jessica sat beside her, staring at the court—apparently she and Richie had broken up over spring break and she was having a hard time getting over it. Kayla was talking to Rosemary, who had pulled her hair back in a studious ponytail. As Kayla yapped, she never took her eyes off the court—like she was suddenly interested in basketball. I couldn't help but think, *Maybe now I actually have something these girls are envious of.*

"Thurman!"

I snapped out of my aren't-you-jealous-of-me reverie and saw a red-faced Coach Eckels across the court.

"Get over here, girl!" he yelled.

I shuffled quickly across the court, heels clomping along the way, hoping Kayla, Jessica and Rosemary didn't hear Coach yelling at me.

I'd never run in heels before, naturally, and had a hard time keeping my balance. I noticed the guys looking at me as I stomped past, and I tried to look as confidently hot as I could.

"Thurman, you on the team now?" Richie called out with a smile as I hobbled by. "You couldn't be much worse than our point guard. He sucks."

I smiled as cute as I could as Shiner yelled, "Shut up, Adams!" Richie laughed as he shot the ball from the free-throw line, missing the basket entirely.

"Camry, get over here!" Coach Eckels hollered at Shiner.

Coach smelled like my dad's deodorant. He was wearing baby blue shorts, the kind with a plastic zipper and two snap buttons on the wide elastic band that all the older coaches wore, a white golf shirt with a Bowie Bandit over the heart, a shiny silver whistle with a light blue rubber tip and a matching lanyard around his neck. With the clipboard in his hand, it was standard coach uniform.

"Dern it, Camry! You watch that mouth of yours around the females, boy. You hear me?" As he yelled, spit gathered in the corner of this mouth. I watched nervously for some of it to fly in my direction.

"Yes, sir," he mumbled, clearly embarrassed.

"Sit down here for the rest of warm-up."

Shiner slumped to the bench with a heavy sigh.

"And no attitude!" Coach Eckels snapped at him.

He turned to me, screwing his eyes up and down, inspecting my outfit.

"What in heaven is this?" he asked, his eyebrows scrunched together.

"I didn't have anything to change into," I explained.

"And what in the gordon-jack-seed is that?" he asked, pointing behind me. There were several black scuffs on the basketball court tracking my path across the court like footsteps in the snow. I groaned and looked down at my discount culprits—betrayed, once again.

"Take those things off," Coach Eckels demanded. "You think this is a beauty pageant?"

"No, sir."

He let out a heavy sigh. "You never wear black soles on a basketball court. Next time wear tennis shoes with white soles, jeans, and I'll give you a shirt. And get here a half hour before game time, Thurman, not five minutes. Got it?"

He directed me to the end of the bench, where the bench-warmers waited, hoping to be called into battle. I took off my boots and tucked them under the bench, exposing my Rudolph socks, while Hector, the guy who filled in for the last stat girl while he sat out on grades probation, showed me what to do and how to keep score. Then he looked down at my socks; the googley-eyed Rudolph ogled up at him.

"Nice," he snickered. I curled my toes in and pulled my feet under my seat while tugging at the hem of my skirt. Insulted by a benchwarmer—not a good start. But then I reminded myself of No. 3 on my list: being nice. So I smiled as genuinely as possible and said, "Thanks, Hector." He snickered in response.

My job was pretty easy. Coach Eckels gave me a clipboard that had a little picture of the basketball court on a piece of paper. When one of the guys made a shot, I wrote his number on the court to mark where he shot from. If the basket went in, I circled his number. In the margins, I wrote down the numbers of the guys who fouled and a notch for each additional foul. I stared at the paper, wondering how many times I'd write down number 32—Jason's number.

"Huddle up!"

All the players ran to the sidelines, where Coach Eckels stood with his hands on his hips. Once they were gathered around him, he looked around frantically.

"Thurman!" he bellowed.

I slid over to him on my socks.

"Where's the ball?"

I stared up at him through unblinking eyes. "Sir?"

"The ball! The ball!" His face turned bright pink, and spit gathered again at the corners of his mouth.

I looked at all the practice balls rolling lazily around the court like lost papers in a breeze and wondered if he wanted me to go get one for him.

"I'll get it," Jason called as he hustled over to the ball rack where one ball remained: The Ball.

How stupid of me to forget. Knowing about The Ball was practically part of the Bowie curriculum, as important as knowing the details of Santa Anna's defeat at San Jacinto. During the day, it sat in the display case at the front entrance to the school with all our trophies and pictures of semifamous people who had gone to our school, like city council members and a Channel 4 news anchor. I passed it every day without even noticing. The Ball was taken out of the case for every game. It was more important than wearing white-soled tennis shoes or knowing the words to our school anthem.

The Ball was used in the 1989 state championship game in which we defeated the Judson Jets. We were crowned state champs for the first, last, and only time so far in Bowie history. Since then we hadn't even made it to the semifinals. In the 1988–89 sports season, Bowie didn't win a single football, baseball, or volleyball game, and our best placement in track was usually a distant third or fourth. But the basketball team exploded because they were led by Enzo Vincenzo, the tallest kid in the county and the best player we'd ever had. He was also one of the dumbest guys around—his bad grades were legendary, but this was before they made the no-pass, no-play rule in Texas schools, so nobody cared how awful his grades were as long as he kept winning games. Enzo scored an average of forty-two points per game, and the final score usually only went up to the sixties. For all practical purposes, he *was* the basketball team.

Enzo led the team to the finals, but three days before the state championship game, he twisted his ankle running down the stairs at his house. They say that when Enzo showed up at school with a cane, teetering down the halls like an old man, teachers stopped and wept. The principal shook his head and said, "We almost made it . . . almost." Coach Randolph, the basketball coach at the time, even considered forfeiting the game rather than sending the team in like soldiers with no weapons.

But the team refused. In the three days they had before the game, they practiced before and after school. The principal even let them out of their sixth- and seventh-period classes so they could go to the gym and start working on new plays. The town was somber: Everyone knew they'd lose, but they loved the boys for their determination. The Bowie basketball team of 1989 was full of martyrs, and the town's collective chest swelled with pride.

The night of the game, all of Ladel traveled to the downtown convention center, including my parents—that was the night they met. My dad was a student at Ladel Senior High, and Mom had driven up from Weatherford High with some friends. They happened to be sitting near each other, my dad with his buddies and my mom with her girlfriends; none of them had ever cared about basketball before that night. The excitement of a championship win filled the hearts of every Ladel citizen. The whole town—even the smaller ones surrounding it—was exhilarated, cheering for these mere boys. By the third period, when the Bandits were leading the game by four points, the whole arena pulsated with the energy of an atom bomb. Mom said it's a wonder she heard a word Dad said to her; it was so loud, you couldn't hear yourself think.

The game went back and forth. The Bandits held a two-point lead, then the Jets. Both teams struggled to pull ahead, and the guys got sloppy with fouls, violently checking one another below the basket. First one of our guys, then one of theirs. People screamed, voices went hoarse. Dad said Mom's cheeks were so pink with excitement that she looked like she'd just met Simon Le Bon of Duran Duran. With forty seconds left on the clock, he asked her out to a movie. Dad joked that she was so caught up in the excitement that she would have said yes to Jack the Ripper. At twenty seconds, Bowie scored a basket that gave us a two-point lead. All we had to do was hold on. But at ten seconds, the Jets threw a sloppy jump shot, which bounced undecidedly on the rim until finally sliding through the net. A great moan came from half the crowd. Hidden in the back of the bleachers was Enzo, a smile snaking onto his face—no way could they make it without him. The crowd slumped, frowns settled on their collective faces, their spirits melted. But the Bandits didn't give up.

The clock ticked down, and the crowd shouted the seconds like it was New Year's Eve.

"Five! Four!"

A kid by the name of Kenny Camry made his way to the half-court line.

"Three! Two!"

He chucked the ball from mid-court just as the buzzer

sounded, and the crowd held its breath. The ball sailed down the court, high in the air. Mom grabbed Dad's hand and squeezed tight, hoping, waiting, until . . .

Swish!

The basket was good, and the crowd exploded into a seismic celebration. Popcorn flew into the air, and no Ladel-loving butt remained in its seat. Mom and Dad jumped and hugged and laughed as if they had just won the lottery, and fans swarmed the court to join the team in their ecstasy. Someone stole the net from the rim, but Coach Randolph scooped up the ball and held it tight, even as the guys dumped ice-cold water over his balding head. No one noticed Enzo Vincenzo slip quietly out the side door. No one ever heard from him again. Rumor is he home-schooled the rest of the year, then transferred to a high school in Angelica Springs. To this day, people debate what became of him. Sometimes you hear of Enzo "sightings," kind of like Elvis, but no one knows for sure where he went or what he did after that night.

Since then, before every basketball game the Bandits play, the head coach gets The Ball and gathers the guys around it in a circle. Everyone piles their hands on top and chants, "Never give up! Fight! Fight! Bandits win! Now!"

Having shamefully forgotten about The Ball, I stood dumbly by as the team repeated the ritual.

Just before the ref blew the whistle to start the game, Coach

Eckels made me clear the stray practice balls off the court and put them in the storage room just off the court. Sounds like an easy job, but I felt ridiculous in my Rudolph-red socks, and bending over in my too-short skirt was not an easy task. I had to kneel straight down in a kind of squat position, pressing my knees together to keep anything from showing in the back or through the front. Ten balls later, my thighs were shaking with exhaustion. Apparently, the *Toning for Teens* I had done over the break hadn't toned me enough.

After wheeling the cart into the supply room, I took my seat at the end of the bench. With Shiner sitting beside me, I readied myself for a stat career I hoped would take me through senior year in high school.

What did I find? Even though I had once tried out for the sport, I have absolutely no interest in basketball other than watching Jason Andersen dribble, do a layup, a free throw, a jump-shot, a pass. His calf muscles looked amazingly complex when he crouched in a low dribble. His hair was matted to his wonderfully pale forehead before the end of the first period, his eyes shined brightly beneath, and his lips looked fuller and rosier from the exertion. When he fouled, he guiltily raised his hand so the scorekeepers—and I—could easily identify him as the culprit of unnecessary roughness. I felt like he was raising his hand to wave, just to me, so I could write it in the little margin on my mini picture of the court.

I also realized that Shiner could actually be sort of cool, in a Shiner kind of way. Since Coach never put him in, he sat at the end of the bench near me. He looked at my clipboard and asked what I was doing. I explained it to him, and when I got bored in the second period, he offered to do them for me.

At half-time, Coach told me to air up the balls in the storeroom and had Shiner show me how to work the air-pumping machine. I guess since he hadn't played, Coach Eckels didn't think Shiner needed to be at the meeting. Of course, Hector got to go to the locker room, and he hadn't played either, so I didn't really understand.

The storeroom was right off the court through a heavy double door, which Shiner held open for me. Metal racks held ceiling-high piles of volleyball knee pads, baseball and softball bats, deflated footballs and volleyballs, beat-up helmets, and buckets full of baseballs. It was a jock's dream in there.

It also stank. It smelled like sweat, dirt, grass, and dirty socks, all rolled into one. The fluorescent light in the back corner of the low ceiling buzzed and flickered anxiously, making the gray walls look like a prison.

Shiner pulled a rusty metal contraption with a long rubber hose down from the shelf and plugged the cord into a socket behind the door.

"Man," I said, feeling the need to fill the silence while I stood around and watched Shiner. "This place is a pit."

"Yeah," he said, looking around the dank room. "Reminds me of my sister's place. Small and stinky." He smiled at me, showing crooked teeth.

"Totally." His sister was three years older than we were, and used to make kissing noises whenever she saw me and Shiner together. She was tall and brash and always intimidated me.

Shiner flicked on the switch, and the pump roared like a ski boat as he showed me how to air the balls.

"You want it full, but not too full!" Shiner shouted over the humming and rattling. "Firm, but not too firm!"

"How will I know?" I yelled back.

"You'll just have to judge! There!" He pulled the needle out of the basketball and turned off the pump. Suddenly I could hear the cheerleaders outside the door doing their half-time routine—a bunch of clapping and stomping. "See?" He spun the orange orb in his palm, then bounced it twice on the concrete floor. "Perfect."

"Thanks, Shiner," I said earnestly.

"No problem." He shuffled in the doorway for a moment, then said, "Hey, look. I'm sorry about today."

"Which part?"

He laughed. "Well, I meant about knocking you in the hall when you were with Coach Eckels. I didn't see him there, but I'm sorry, anyway. It was a jerk thing to do."

I can honestly say that I thought that Shiner Camry would

never bother to apologize to me for anything, especially since I never apologized to him for abruptly ending our Fall Ball dance. I was impressed, to say the least. "God, that was the least of my problems today," I said. "But, thanks. It's okay. I mean, you don't have to apologize."

He shrugged. "I wish I'd told you about Mrs. Everly's outfit earlier. I saw her walking across the parking lot this morning. That's actually why I came up to you in the hall—to tell you. That's just like me to try to do something nice then mess it all up."

He put his hand on the handle of the door but didn't open it. We stood quietly for a moment, the cheers of the half-time routine coming through the walls muffled.

"Hey," I called as he started to open the door. "You're good at basketball. I remember you used to like to play. How come you're not playing now?"

He shrugged his bony shoulders. "I don't think Coach likes me very much."

There wasn't much I could say to that because it was probably true. Shiner always rubbed people the wrong way. I think no one really gave him a chance anymore. "Hey, was that your dad who played during the game in eighty-nine? Kenny Camry?"

"Yeah."

"Really?" I wondered why more people didn't realize

it was Shiner's dad. "What ever happened to him? I mean, I know he had you and your folks split when we were little, but did he keep playing ball?"

Shiner opened the door and let the screaming crowd and cheerleaders into our tiny space. "No," he said, an edge to his voice. "He decided to become a burned-out loser instead."

I sighed as he left. I stuck the needle in the little rubber opening and flicked on the switch like Shiner had shown me and wondered if someone like Jason could ever go for someone like me. If you could have someone like Kayla or especially Rosemary, then why would you go for a period-roses, Kotex-locker, old-lady-clothes-wearing, Class Favorite wannabe who . . .

I didn't hear the explosion exactly. Not right away. In fact, I didn't hear anything. The whole world went silent, like someone had pressed a giant mute button. Then the ringing started. . . .

One moment the basketball was resting in my hand, the needle inserted like an IV, the pump humming like white noise in the background of my thoughts, and then . . .

Full but not too full, Shiner had told me.

I was shaking. Not just my hands—which no longer held the ball—but my entire body. Uncontrollable, violent shaking, like I was standing at the epicenter of an earthquake. Next I heard a noise—a buzzing/ringing in my ears that sounded like the emergency broadcast signal the TV stations sometimes tested, except this ringing drowned out all other sounds. It was quiet at first, building, and then it was all I could hear.

Firm but not too firm, Shiner had instructed.

I looked at my shaking hands, then down at the concrete floor, where the ball was blown into four oblong pieces. I knew I wasn't hurt, exactly—my limbs all seemed to be intact, and there wasn't any blood that I could see. Still, I didn't understand immediately what I'd done. It was that weird feeling of waking up in the middle of a dream—I paused for a moment, waiting to see what was real.

The ringing in my ears continued, but after a moment—a minute? five minutes?—I started to hear what was going on outside the door in the gym. Part of the ringing in my ears wasn't from the explosion of the ball, it was screaming. Girls were screaming, and I could hear a low rumbling, like a stampede. But I still couldn't budge.

Suddenly I was aware that something was on my arm—a veiny hand attached to a long skinny arm. Shiner. As I looked at him I realized how wide open my right eye was, and that the left was twitching uncontrollably. His mouth was moving frantically, but I couldn't hear a word he said. I just stared at him like I was comatose or something.

"Hey! Sara!" He shook me gently. "Are you okay? Sara?"

"Y-y-y . . . yes . . . yeah. I'm . . . fine."

"Geez, was that you?"

I stared at him, finally aware of my mouth hanging open.

"Sara, take a breath, come on." Shiner demonstrated for me by breathing deeply once, twice . . . I managed to follow his lead and took a long, deep breath, which I never knew could feel so good. I didn't realize that I hadn't even been breathing. By my third breath, I felt much calmer and was able to relax my shoulders and turn my Rudolph stocking feet to face him. I couldn't stop shaking, the ringing continued, and the pump hummed ominously in front of me.

"Was that you?" he asked again as he yanked the cord out of the wall, the sound of the pump stopping instantly while a steady ringing continued in my ears. "Did you . . ." Then he looked down and caught sight of the basketball. "Ah, hell, Thurman." The concern vanished from his face, and he actually started to laugh. Shaking his head and laughing that high-pitched squeal of his, he bent over and put his hands on his knees, his back convulsing.

"You blew up a basketball?" he finally asked. "That's it? That's what happened?"

"Yeah," I said, calmer now and, quite frankly, confused because he was laughing at my traumatic mistake. "I guess I wasn't paying attention."

"Oh man, Thurman. You really did it this time. Man, this just ain't your week. Ain't your *month*. Shoot, I didn't know a basketball exploding could be so loud. But, man, it is. You've cleared out the whole . . ." he started laughing again. "You've got the whole . . . oh, man, this is too good. . . ."

"What? *Shiner.* What's so funny?"

"You've got the whole gym cleared out. Everyone thought it was a bomb, it was so loud. The cheerleaders, they started screaming, and Kayla Cane screamed, 'Bomb!'" He demonstrated this in an oddly high voice that sounded nothing like Kayla's. "Man, you should have seen it. It was a total stampede! Everyone is out on the football field right now. Nice work, Thurman."

"Oh, my God," I muttered, looking down at the exploded ball. "Oh, my God. This is just great. I'm going to get in so much trouble. Coach Eckels is going to be so mad. . . ."

"Ah, calm down," he said, taking a step toward me and resting his hand on my back. "It's not *that* big a deal. You're probably not the first person to explode a ball."

The door flew open. Coach Eckels pounced in frantically, his tanned skin a blushed pink. "What's going on? What happened?"

Shiner stepped back from me as if we were doing something wrong, and I dumbly pointed down to the torn leather at my feet. "I'm sorry. I blew it up."

"My Lord," Coach said, running his hand through his thick white hair, looking both relieved and annoyed. "You okay, Sara?"

"Yes, sir," I said with a shaky voice.

"I think she's just a little shook up," Shiner offered. Coach Eckels looked quickly over at him—I guess he hadn't noticed him standing there.

"Well, all right then," Coach was saying, looking down at the ball. "Camry, go outside and tell Coach Wendell everything is fine. Tell him what happened and to bring everyone back in."

Shiner scrambled out the door, and Coach looked at me.

"They called in the police. Everyone thought it was a bomb."

"I know. I'm sorry. I didn't mean to."

"You okay?"

"I guess. I think there's something in my eye, and my ears are ringing."

"We'll get Coach Wendell to take you to the hospital, get you checked out." He let out a big sigh and a little laugh. "Whew! You had us scared there, Thurman. I thought it was some crazy ex-student, back for revenge; maybe ol' Enzo finally came back to show us. Well, so long as you're okay. A basketball can certainly be replaced. After all," he chuckled, "it's not as if you blew up The Ball."

My eyes widened, and I felt sickness creeping up in my throat. Still, I gave a little laugh, then asked, "How can you tell if it's The Ball?"

He bent down and picked up the pieces. "Well, we didn't want to put a bunch of writing on The Ball, you know, mess it all up." As he spoke he examined the orange and black scraps of leather. "So old Coach Randolph"—his eyebrows scrunched together—"put a little '#1' right . . . by . . . the . . ."

♥14♥

Does He Like You . . . Like That?

Testing the waters, you tell your friend and heart's desire, Stefan, that the new guy in history is totally cute. He:

a) scoffs and says, "You can do better!"

b) nods and says, "Yeah, he's like the female version of that smokin' Brazilian babe in our homeroom."

c) doesn't even look up, just mumbles, "Whatever."

When Coach Eckels saw that little #1 by the black rubber insertion thing, he went totally ballistic. Suddenly he didn't care that I was okay, or even that I really *wasn't* okay because my eye was twitching more and more with every curse word Coach Eckels tossed around the storage room, despite his policy of not cursing around "the womenfolk." He eventually told me to get out of his sight, which I did, and gladly.

Coach Wendell drove me to East Side Memorial to get

my eyes and ears checked out. He sat with me in the waiting room while we waited for a doctor to see me and for my mom to come get me. He didn't say anything, just sighed and scratched the back of his head a lot, then rested his hands back on the rounded belly that spilled over his coach shorts. The silence made me so anxious for a word of encouragement that I finally couldn't take it anymore.

"Coach Wendell, I'm so sorry," I implored. "I didn't mean to do it."

He sighed again as he stared off at the muted TV high up in the corner of the room. "Well . . . I wouldn't worry too much about it. I'm sure it's . . . well, there's nothing much we can do about it now." He never even looked at me.

If anyone should be upset, it should have been me. After all, that Ball inspired my existence. If Bowie hadn't won that game in 1989, my dad might never have summoned the courage to ask my mom out—he might not have even noticed her in the first place. But when I went daydreaming about some boy (even a totally lusty boy), I let The Ball—my existence—explode into four ripped pieces. One for each member of my broken family. How nauseatingly poetic.

An eternity later, Mom showed up looking disheveled. Her hair hung as if exhausted against her cheeks, her ears poking through.

"Good God, Sara," she said, tilting my chin up so she

could look at my twitching eye. She took in my outfit, cocked an eyebrow, and asked, "What happened now?" Her mascara had run a bit with the long day, and her blouse was slightly untucked beneath her skirt.

Out of the corner of my good eye, I could see Coach Wendell shaking his head.

"I accidentally blew up the basketball at half-time."

"It wasn't The Ball, was it?"

Didn't I say the story was legendary? I could only look down at the floor.

"Sara!" she gasped. "Not *The* Ball?"

When she said that, I started to cry. There I was in my too-short skirt and clunky boots, the green-ish lights of the waiting room casting weird shadows on everyone's faces. I felt like the kid who always gets picked on at school, except the only person picking on me was . . . me. I had wanted to blame my bad situations on someone else ever since the day I got the roses, but there in the hospital, I realized it was all on me.

I bawled, and Mom immediately pulled me to her shoulder as Coach Wendell slipped discreetly toward the vending machines.

"Oh, honey," Mom said. "Hush, now." She squeezed me tight.

Up to that point, the only person who had genuinely tried to tell me it was okay was Shiner—which made me want to cry even harder. I wanted Arlene to be the one who said it was going to be all right. Kirstie had been a good friend to me so far, but she wasn't my best friend—nothing could replace Arlene. She would have calmed me down after the blow-up and then would have made me laugh about the whole thing. Arlene would have told me it was just a stupid ball. I missed her. I felt betrayed, but I still missed her.

And poor Mom. Standing there in her heinous Dress Barn clothes she'd had since Elisabeth was a toddler. The black and white blouse was coarse and nubbly, and I couldn't imagine that she had once considered it nice enough to buy. The last time I remember her getting all dressed up was the time she and Dad went to the Bighorn Sheep Foundation dinner a couple of years ago. They had come home laughing and talking loudly, waking me up. Mom's diamond necklace had tickled my face when she bent to kiss me good night, and she had held her high heels in her manicured hand.

"It's gonna be fine," Mom assured me back in the waiting room. "Don't you worry about a thing."

Those simple words made me feel better. I'd blown up The Ball and that was it. Just like Coach Wendell had said: There wasn't much we could do about it now. What was done, was done. I'd probably get expelled tomorrow, so let's just get on with it.

My life had become one of amazing highs and dreadful lows, and I hardly had time to recover from the pain or properly bask in the joy before something else was hitting me in the face.

Two hours after I arrived at East Side Memorial, I was discharged. Nothing was wrong with me, physically. The doctor who blessed me with his medical genius shined a light in my eye and didn't find anything wrong with it. I had probably rinsed out whatever was in there when I sobbed on Mom's shoulder. Still, he gave me some drops to put in for the next forty-eight hours in case it was still sensitive. As for the ringing in my ears, he shined a light in them, too, and told me there wasn't any permanent damage but if the ringing didn't go away within twenty-four hours to go see my regular doctor. The whole thing took less than five minutes. But he did take time to chuckle when I told him I had blown up a basketball. He abruptly stopped chuckling when Mom added, "*The* Ball."

I stood bored next to Mom as she filled out the insurance papers. She scribbled in my social security number, which I had yet to memorize, and reached over and patted my back—not making a show of it but just doing it.

Then something amazing, wonderful, exciting, perfect happened. The automatic doors of the emergency entrance opened, and beauty was wheeled in.

"Oh, my gosh, what happened to you?" I asked, stepping away from Mom.

Jason smiled as his mother, who was tall like him, and so

elegant in her straight black pants and heels, wheeled him through the door in a wheelchair, his leg propped up and wrapped in a bandage at the ankle.

"Infamous Ball Girl," he said, a bright smile on his face. "You okay?"

"Shoot, I'm fine," I said, trying to act breezy.

"You caused a real scene tonight. I'm surprised you didn't give yourself a heart attack."

"I wish."

Mrs. Andersen went to the desk next to my mother to check Jason in. Our moms said hello to each other, and the differences in their appearance was stark: a princess and a pauper.

"Well, what happened to you?" I asked, motioning to his propped-up leg.

"Came down wrong on a jump shot."

"Does it hurt?"

"Just sort of a steady throbbing. Not too bad."

"You don't seem too upset about it."

He shrugged his shoulders. "Why should I be?"

Was he crazy? Basketball helped make him what he was today, socially speaking. Without basketball, it was possible he'd morph back into the meek kid he had been all through elementary school. Or maybe, I thought, once you reached the top, it was hard to fall back down? I realized that I had no one thing that would take me to the top of the Bowie social scene, but

I had my list that I was slowly trudging through. Maybe with the right clothes and attitude, I would at least get some positive attention.

"Well, I mean, you're only one of the best players on the team. What are we gonna do if you're out for the season?"

"Eh," he said. "There's only a couple of games left, and I'm no Enzo. I don't think it's going to be that big a deal, to tell you the truth."

"How come?"

"You're friends with Shiner, right?"

For a moment, I hesitated. Maybe he was going to say something bad about Shiner and then I'd look like his co-loser if I was associated with him. But then I thought, *What do I care?* Shiner's not as bad as I thought he was—not as bad as Kayla had me thinking he was. So I said, "Yeah, we're sort of friends."

"Well, it turns out he's an awesome basketball player."

"Really?" I asked, but I had guessed that already.

"Man, you should have seen it. I hurt my ankle late in the third period, but I stuck around on the bench once they put Shiner in and he started tearing it up on the court."

"Coach Eckels actually put him in?"

"He could have put Hector in, but he didn't. It was the right decision. Just shows what an awesome coach he is," Jason beamed. "He knew exactly when to use that guy, knew exactly when he'd be mature enough to play. But, anyway, you should have seen it. Shiner scored fourteen points in the last period. I mean, we probably would have won, anyway, but he was awesome, like his dad used to be. Really great."

"Wow," I said, stunned. "Pretty cool."

"Yeah," he said, looking to his mom, who was waving him over.

"Looks like you get to move to the head of the line," I said. "I had to wait for, like, two hours."

"Possible breaks always get priority over shell shock." He grinned. "Guess I better go."

"I hope your ankle is okay."

"It'll be fine." He began wheeling himself away, then stopped and said, "Hey, Sara, listen. I'm having a party next weekend, a bunch of people are gonna be there. My parents included, so, you know, it's not one of those parties. But it'd be cool if you stopped by."

Okay. This just was not possible. Not only had Jason already approached me in the halls unsolicited, but now he was asking me to his party. Me to his party! These things just do not happen in real life—I actually pinched my arm to make sure I wasn't having some random narcoleptic episode. I was wide awake, though, and beginning to see my name on that ballot.

"Yeah," I heard myself saying, my insides bursting with excitement, a little squeal of exhilaration squeaking out of my mouth. "That'd be cool."

Back at home, Elisabeth was stretching on the floor of the living room, her face pink and wet, the back of her Revlon 5K T-shirt sweated through.

"Dad called," she said.

"He did?" Mom and I both said this at the same time. When I looked at Mom, she had the same expectant face that I was sure I wore: excited that he had called, agitated that we had missed it. *Does she think he was calling for her?* I thought. Which made me wonder, Was *he calling for her?*

Elisabeth had the same surprised look that I had. She looked at me and said, "Yeah, Sara. And he sent us a package. It's on the dining room table."

As I ran into the kitchen, I hollered back, "Is he calling back? Where is he?"

"Oklahoma City, and I don't know."

"Well, didn't you talk to him?"

"I didn't recognize the caller ID, so I let voice mail get it."

The brown paper package lay ripped and shredded on the kitchen table, quickly reminding me of the way The Ball had looked lying at my feet. I pushed that thought out of my mind as I dug through the scraps looking for the treasure beneath.

There was one of those snow globes you can shake up and watch the snow fall on a tiny village, except this one was rubbery instead of glass, like I imagined a fake boob would be.

Inside was the top half of the state of Texas and the bottom of Arkansas and Louisiana. In the center, where the three states came together, stood a little girl with a pink bow waving at me. It read: TEXARKANA WELCOMES YOU! I gave it the obligatory shake and watched the glitter float down like a surprise party. It was cute and all, but I wished my dad would realize I wasn't eight. I wanted some real gifts: spa beauty kits, new purses, a season pass to Six Flags.

I set the glitter ball aside and dug through the papers again until I found an envelope with my name on it. As soon as I saw my dad's handwriting, my heart gave a little lurch. Mom used to say that Dad had the prettiest handwriting of any man she'd ever met. I grabbed the envelope and carefully opened it as I sat down in a chair.

Sara,

I got you and your sister little gifts from the road. I always told you that there's nothing good to buy out there on my routes, but I thought these were kind of fun. You and your sister can choose between the two—don't fight over them, though! Be sweet to each other.

I sure do miss my girls like crazy! I want y'all to know that, even though I don't see you so often, I'm thinking of you all the time. If there's one thing being on the road lets you do, that's <u>think</u>. I do more thinking out here than I ever thought I could stand. I think about my girls and how fast you're growing up. You're going to start dating soon, I suppose. I try not to think about that.

I been thinking a lot about our talk at Luby's. I know school is hard, and kids are hard on one another. But you always got to stick by your best friends. I'm not sure if you and Arlene are having a hard time of it, but I hope that if something isn't right with the two of you that you'll take the first step in making it right—no matter whose fault it is. When I was in high school there was a kid who had it in for me real bad, and no matter what I did or didn't do, it seemed like he would pounce on me for it. But my buddy Harlin was always there for me to vent to at the end of the day. You and Arlene have been friends forever (remember how you used to make homemade doughnuts!) and I'd hate to see you just give that up. Don't be like me and your momma and let something stupid get in the way of something great.

Oh, I almost forgot! I put a calling card in this envelope so that you can call me on my cell free of charge anytime you want. It won't cost you a cent. Promise me you'll call me if there's anything you want, anything at all. Okay?

I love you girls more than anything! Be sweet to your momma, and I'll try to call you when I get to Oklahoma City.

Love,
Dad

I gently folded the letter and placed it back in its envelope. Elisabeth's envelope lay haphazardly torn on the mess of brown paper. I looked inside to see if her letter was still in there, but the envelope was empty.

"Everything okay?" Mom asked. She was leaning in the doorway; I wondered how long she'd been standing there.

"Dad gave a me a calling card. Said I could call anytime."

"You want me to show you how to use it?" she asked eagerly.

I looked at my mother and wondered what was going on inside her head. Did she miss Dad? I smiled at her as she alternately looked at me and the envelope that held Dad's letter. "No thanks, Mom. I'll figure it out."

The truth was, I wasn't ready to call Dad just yet. Or Arlene or even Kirstie. I just wanted to go to my room and read the letter again and shake the fake boob ball and watch the girl from Texarkana wave at me while I tried to figure out why everything had to be so complicated when things used to be so simple.

♥15♥

What's Your Rep?

You just won an award for Most Conscientious Recycler in your town. How does your school respond?

a) By surprising you with a full-page ad in the local paper congratulating you

b) It doesn't. Only your two closest friends know, because they're the only ones you told.

c) It doesn't, but at least your parents are proud of you.

The day after "the incident," as it would come to be known, I knew that damage control was crucial. When I looked at my Class Favorite list, I figured poise (No. 5) would be important. Haden Prescott totally kept her head high after a very public break-up with that financier guy, and all the weeklies showed her laughing and lunching with her girlfriends. Killing The Ball was tragic, I decided, but not the end of the world. I did feel a bit defeated, but I reminded myself that I was on track toward my goal, and at Jason's party I intended to seal the deal.

I felt wiser than I had been the day before, realizing how silly my sexy school girl outfit was, so I chose an outfit that was much more low-key: I wore jeans and a striped button-down. The outfit still complied with my Class Favorite list—I had a Rosemary-chic thing going on. I had a couple more hot-looking outfits I'd scrounged up over spring break, but I decided to save one of those for Jason's party . . . *which I'd been personally invited to, thank you very much*. My Class Favorite pipe dream just might become a reality.

I walked to first-period English feeling awesome, despite blowing up The Ball—a guy like Jason Andersen can do that to a girl. But then, I saw Arlene. She stood outside the classroom talking to Ellen Spitz. I couldn't imagine, outside of softball, what they had in common. I wondered how close they had become in the last few weeks and if Arlene talked to her about me. It was weird that Ellen, who I'd never even thought about before, was now best friends with my best friend—*former*.

I bolted by them and tried to pick up just a tiny bit of their conversation, but they stopped talking when they saw me.

I slid into my seat and waited for Jason to walk through the door. When he finally hobbled in, my heart gave an anxious little leap, and I tried to look as normal and unconcerned as possible. I really wanted to throw up.

"Man, Andersen, what's your problem?" said Sean Hurley as Jason lumbered to his seat in one of those walking casts. "You let those Rebels do this to you? They suck; I thought you were good," he teased.

"Yeah, well how many points did *you* score, Hurley?"

I knew that Jason had scored eight points and Sean had only scored four in the first half of the game.

"Oh my," Sean squealed in a voice that was presumably supposed to sound like a girl, hugging his hands to his chest and fluttering his eyes. "What we will ever do without our Golden Boy? We might as well end the season now."

"Screw you, Hurley," Jason said with a crooked smile. "Besides, I think there's a new Golden Boy, anyway."

Amazing, right? Shiner wasn't even trying, and he was ascending the social ranks of our school quicker than I was. He had an actual talent, though, whereas I was trying to get by on my questionable looks and charm.

"Everybody please settle down and get your books out," commanded Ms. Galarza as she moved toward the front of the room and started handing out worksheets. I shifted in my seat, wishing Jason would look at me. When he turned to hand the stack of worksheets to the girl behind him, I glanced at him and caught his eye; he smiled and mouthed, *Hey*. I smiled eagerly back. I wanted to ask him how his ankle was, but he faced the front of the class as Ms. Galarza started talking. Then an announcement came on the intercom.

"Good morning, Bowie Bandits. This is Principal Moran. Sorry to interrupt your classes, but as some of you may already be aware, we lost a very important part of our school's history last night. Something that represented the will and pride of our great school." The class shuffled and whispered, and I tried to hide behind my textbook. "The Ball of the nineteen eighty-nine state championship game has been erroneously destroyed."

Some of the girls in the class—the few who hadn't been at the game or heard word—gave out a little gasp; there were murmurs throughout the room, and a couple of people gave me accusatory looks. I slumped down in my seat and eagerly looked at the worksheet.

"Though The Ball is now gone, we mustn't ever forget its spirit, for that lives on forever in the heart of every true Bandit. Now, I'd like to request three minutes of silence for our lost comrade."

Three whole minutes? One minute of complete quiet is horrible enough, but *three*? The silence was excruciating. Most people bowed their heads, as if they were praying—actually *praying*—for a basketball. Some people started giving me backward glances, and I figured they might as well have propped me up on a stage and let people hurl rotten fruit and insults at me. After what was probably the first minute, people started getting restless, shuffling in their seats and sighing with great fanfare. Somebody coughed, "Ballbuster," which set off a round of stifled laughs while Ms. Galarza gently shushed us, her eyes cast down but occasionally cutting at those making noise. I risked a look at Arlene; our eyes locked for a moment, and I thought I saw sympathy in her eyes. I looked away, embarrassed.

Finally, after what seemed like the entire class period, Mr. Moran came back on the intercom and said somberly, "Thank you, students. Have a pleasant day."

I darted out of class as soon as the bell rang, eager for an escape. No amount of poise or perceived confidence could keep me from feeling humiliated all over again.

"Sara! Hey, wait up."

Like a magical spell, the sound of my name oozing out of Jason's lips temporarily erased those feelings of utter humiliation. I turned to face him with, hopefully, a very beautiful gaze plastered on my face while a voice inside my head screamed that this was the second time he had approached me on his own.

"Where you headed?" he asked. "I'll limp with you." He smiled, and just like that, I forgot all about that stupid announcement.

"Can you believe Mr. Moran and that insanely ridiculous announcement?" he asked—so much for forgetting. "Three minutes? I mean, could he have been more dramatic? It's just a *ball.*" *Exactly!* I thought. "I mean, sure, it means a lot to some people and represents the potential in all of us, but still, get over it, right?"

"Yeah, I guess," I said as we neared the front office. I cringed when I saw that the trophy case still displayed The Ball, only now it held the strips of torn leather as the overhead spotlight shined defiantly on. I was starting to realize that it takes real mental and emotional strength to act like you don't care, or that it doesn't bother you. Still, I said, "Well, you know, what the heck am I supposed to do? It's not like I did it on purpose. I know The Ball was a big deal and all, but . . ."

"What's done is done, right?"

I smiled back at him. "Right. Look, thanks, but you don't have to walk with me." Of course, I totally wanted him to keep walking with me, but not at the risk of permanent bone damage. With a glance down at his leg, I asked, "How's your ankle, anyway?"

"It's okay," he said, giving a heads up to Richie Adams.

"Hey!" Richie called to us both. "Grace Thurman strikes again!"

And instead of trying to morph into the walls, I said, "That's me!" Loud and proud, even as I died inside. As Richie passed the trophy case, he jokingly crossed himself.

"Anyway," Jason continued, "I'll have this thing on for five weeks, though, which sucks. No more basketball for me this year."

"Are you bummed?"

He hesitated, then said, "Yeah. I guess so. There's only two more games in the season, anyway. Maybe you're right about the walk," he said as we approached the glass doors leading out to the courtyard and across to the other side of the school. "I should probably cut across here, get off this ankle."

"Okay. I guess I'll see you in algebra."

"Yeah, see you then. Hey," he said, "how are you doing on those equations, anyway?"

"Not so good, actually. I'm pretty good at solving them through elimination, but the substitution thing keeps tripping me up."

"Huh, that's funny," he said. "I'm just the opposite. Substitutions are a breeze for me, but man, I hate solving by elimination."

"Really?" I wondered how I could possibly be better than him at anything. And how could he not know how to do the eliminations? They're so easy!

"Listen," he began. "This might sound kind of lame but, you want to maybe help each other out with it? We've got that exam next week you know."

Holy freaking crap. *Help each other out?* I'm not an expert on guys' language, but that was a total ask-out. Sure, it's an algebra date—not exactly romantic, but . . . then I realized I hadn't responded. "I know, I'm totally dreading it."

"You want to meet in the library after school? We don't

have basketball practice since there was a game last night."

"Oh, well, yeah then. That'd be cool."

"Cool. Then I guess I'll see you in class, anyway."

I could feel bursts of happiness beaming from my face. Studying with Jason Andersen—that took care of Nos. 6 and 4 on my list: working on my grades and getting a boyfriend. How perfect was that? And I didn't need some schoolgirl outfit to grab his attention. Destroying our school's relic was a small price to pay.

As I turned to go up the hall, past the courtyard, I thought it'd be cool to flip my hair all flirty-like to give Jason something to remember during his next class. And instead of accidentally banging my forehead on a door or something, I got it just right. I tossed my hair over my shoulder, gave him my best million-buck smile, and said, "See ya."

I was totally dying. After school I dug in my locker nervously as Kirstie lazily twisted her hair into a spiral and then let it unwind.

"Relax, girl," she said. "This is a good thing—don't ruin the moment by freaking out."

"I know, I know. You're right." *Be poised,* I thought. *Be confident.* After seeing Jason I had searched the halls for Kirstie to tell her what happened. I wondered what Arlene would think of my change of luck.

"You got your list?" she asked.

"Never leave home without it. Although, I'm not sure why—I have the whole thing memorized."

"It's good to have it, though, just as a reminder," Kirstie said.

"I'm going to show him a little one, five, six, and seven!"

After Kirstie shoved me along, I made a pit stop in the bathroom to get gorgeous, but realized that I didn't have any makeup or even a brush in my bag. Instead, I combed my fingers through my hair and tried pinching my cheeks à la Scarlett O'Hara (which hurt like heck for what good it did), then used the pay phone by the front office to call Mom at work, letting her know I'd be a little late.

"Just make sure you're home for dinner," she cheered.

When I got to the library after school, I looked around anxiously for Jason, feeling totally exposed standing in the doorway. All afternoon I had avoided thinking about being alone in a quiet place with Jason Andersen and the hundreds of things that could go wrong . . . or right. But as I stood in the doorway of the library, wondering if he would even show, I knew I had to be cool—as in not such a freak—for once in my life. Then, a set of hands grabbed me around my waist, surprising me into making this really horrible high-pitched squeal. Jason laughed and said, "I guess you're ticklish," and I could feel my cheeks flush hot with the feel of his hands on me.

"Excuse you, children," said Mrs. Franklin, the librarian. "But please keep it down. And no screaming?" She said it like a question, her hefty figure perched permanently on a high chair behind the desk as if she hadn't stopped stamping due dates since Tom Hanks last made a comedy.

"Sorry," I whispered to her.

Jason laughed again and said, "Come on, Sara," and I followed him to a back table, near the U.S. and world history section and by the window that looked out on the courtyard he had crossed earlier in the day.

When we sat down, Jason immediately began rubbing his leg just above where the cast ended. "This thing is killing me," he said. "It throbs like crazy."

I shuffled in my bag for my algebra book and notebook. As I opened my notebook, a loose piece of paper went fluttering out—my Class Favorite qualities list. I sucked in my breath, and tried to snatch it before it hit the floor. If Jason saw it, it'd be over forever. I was so spazzed to get the list just before it landed that, as I bent to catch it, I slammed my head on the edge of the table. I didn't feel the pain until the paper was safely in my hands—facedown—and was jammed into my bag that I realized Jason was laughing. "Stop laughing," I said, rubbing my forehead.

"Never a dull moment, Sara. Not one." He gave a final chuckle and shook his head, looking down at his book. "Well, I guess we should start. I've got all night."

"Actually," I said, rubbing my forehead, "my mom wants me home for dinner."

"Yeah? That's cool. I didn't think families actually had dinner together anymore." He rubbed the spot just above his boot again, his eyes focused down on his unopened book.

"It's my mom's idea. She thinks it's, like, important or something for us to eat together since she and my dad split. I don't know what good it does."

Jason stopped rubbing and stared over at my open book. "Hmm . . . yeah, I know what you mean," he said, then thoughtfully added, "Which do you think is the worst: the fighting or the silence?"

"Me? I don't know. I guess if it's quiet, at least my sister isn't saying something stupid to me or my mom isn't mad at me for something I did." I didn't realize his parents were divorced, and was glad that we had something in common.

"True," Jason said, tapping his pencil on his notebook. "But don't you hate that kind of silence when no one is saying anything but it's like everyone knows what everyone else is thinking? And you're all trying to avoid looking at one another but you can't help making glances around, anyway? And then, if you ask someone to pass the iced tea, everyone jumps up at once like they've been waiting there to serve you the whole time? You know what I mean?"

I thought about it for a moment; I could see what he

meant, although I never really saw my parents fight—they just ignored each other.

"Did your parents fight a lot or something?" I asked.

He sighed. "Constantly fighting, either by yelling or ignoring each other. When they're doing the silent thing, I think they think they're doing me and my sister a huge favor by not screaming at each other. But it's just as bad."

I stared down at the table and said, "Before my parents split, they used to tell me and my sister to go outside to play when they were about to break into a big fight. My sister would dare me to stand underneath their bedroom window and listen to what they were fighting about. And then, when they called us back inside and my dad huffed and Mom sighed more than usual, it was so obvious what had been going on. If they were actors, they'd totally win a Razzie for best worst performance."

"A what?" he asked, a smile forming on his lips.

"Oh," I said, having forgotten myself. "The Golden Raspberry. It's this award thing for the worst movies and actors. It's kind of funny. Arlene and I used to rent really bad movies and watch them just to laugh at how awful they are. Anyway." I immediately realized that I had spoken of Arlene in the past tense, like she was this friend I once had but never would again. Even though we hadn't spoken in so long, I had never fully believed that we would never be friends again. It was something I wasn't sure I'd ever be able to accept. But I couldn't think about her then, though. I'd start crying for sure. "Is it better in your house with just your mom?"

Jason rubbed his hand across his forehead, and I noticed that his nails were cut properly, not all bitten down to the skin like most boys'. "I don't know. Since Dad moved out, Mom tries to be real nice to all of us. It's like she's trying too hard sometimes. I think that's why she's letting me have the party."

"Sounds exactly like my mom. I mean, hello? The roses?" I couldn't believe I had just willingly brought up one of my most embarrassing moments to Jason. "Talk about trying too hard."

He laughed and said, "Point taken. You definitely win on that front."

We sat for a moment, and then, to kill the silence, I said, "So. Do you want to try to do these problems at the end of the chapter?"

He gave a little groan and flipped open his algebra book. "Yeah, sure. Equations, equations, equations. . . ," he muttered as he thumbed through his textbook. "Let's do the substitutions first since you have to leave."

I took a deep breath. "Okay, but don't make fun of how little I know. I mean, aren't these things impossible to do unless you're a total genius?"

"Nah. You just have to make sure you do each step of the formula, and you're set."

"Er . . . there's a formula to these things?"

He nudged me with his good foot. "Sara, you crack me up."

As we sat together in the library going over our algebra—Jason was right: It was easy once you got the formula down—I realized that I wasn't so nervous around him anymore. He was a guy just like anyone else. Except he had chosen me, Nobody Sara Thurman, to do homework with while confessing dark family secrets.

Which made me wonder: *Is it possible that I'm not as bad as I thought?*

♥ **16** ♥

Be Honest: Do You Love, Like, or Hate Gossip?

You have just been told that your economics teacher, Mr. Russo, has been performing in a play downtown. What do you do?

a) You e-mail the entire school directory with the news, including the when/where/cost of the play, and try to rally everyone to go see him—it'll be a huge laugh!

b) You tell your closest friends, giggle about it, but wonder if it's true.

c) You shrug off the information—there's nothing to back up its truth, and besides, even if it *is* true, he's still an awesome teacher.

Over the next few days, I bounded into school with renewed energy. Suddenly I didn't feel so lethargic. Thanks to the sort-of date I'd had with Jason and the fact that he had invited me to his party, I realized he wasn't as untouchable as I had thought. He was just a boy. Who happened to be maddeningly gorgeous, but still.

Later that day I spotted Rosemary and Kayla standing by the vending machine outside the cafeteria just as I was going in to meet Kirstie. I thought of No. 8 on my Class Favorite list: friends. I was beginning to think of ways Arlene and I could reconcile (and I knew it would have to begin with me), but in the meantime, hanging with two of the most popular girls—even if one of them wasn't exactly my number-one fan—would help propel me even closer to my goal. We could hang out together at Jason's party, and by Monday after the party, surely we'd all be passing notes in algebra. Looking at them, I thought, *Rosemary Vickers is not so much better than me, right?* Besides, if Adam Sandler could bounce back in movies after *Little Nicky*—one of the last Golden Raspberries Arlene and I had watched—then I could come back from my own momentous disasters. If I were actually a Class Favorite nominee instead of just channeling their traits, then I would embrace No. 7 on my list—confidence—and walk right up to these girls and get in the conversation. So that's what I did.

"Hi, Rosemary. What's up, Kayla?" I said confidently as I approached them, telling myself I had every right to talk to them. Maybe they should have intimidated me—they were *it,* after all—but for some reason, they didn't. At least, I didn't let them. I'd always felt that Rosemary had this very open, real quality about her. Kind of like Haden Prescott: how, even if you'd never spoken to her, you could tell she was just as sweet in real life as she was in interviews and movies.

Rosemary stopped talking, and Kayla cut her eyes at me.

"Hey," I said again, with a push of determination.

"What's up, Sally?" Kayla said, eyeing me.

"Sara," I breezily corrected. "Not much. Just about to head into the barfeteria. Meat loaf today?"

"Not sure," Rosemary said as Kayla flipped her thick hair back and shifted in her strappy sandals. "I never buy." She held up a gingham cloth bag cinched closed with a pink satin ribbon.

"Oh, cool. Good choice," I blabbed. Conversation wasn't exactly flowing, but I wasn't leaving until it was dead in the water.

"Actually," Kayla began, "we were talking about you earlier."

"Oh. Really?" My mind zipped. Was it already around school that Jason Andersen and Sara Thurman recently had had a library date? Or that he had *personally* invited me to his party and we were now practically a couple? Maybe they were talking about putting me on the Class Favorite ballot because I was so *worthy*. . . .

"Was it really you who blew up The Ball?" Kayla asked.

Kerplunk went my heart.

"Uh . . . well, yeah." *Maintain calm, maintain calm.* I told myself that any publicity was good publicity.

"Oh, my God," Kayla shrieked. "That night was so insane. I can't believe it! And it was *you?*"

I meekly shrugged my shoulders.

"Geez, Kay." Rosemary looked at me and rolled her eyes. "Calm down."

Kayla's wide eyes were filled with excitement. "That was only the single greatest event of the entire year. It was," she concluded, "beyond hilarious."

"Oh . . . really?"

"We were just saying how embarrassed we would have been if it were us," Rosemary said. "But you seem to, I don't know, sort of take it all in stride. You don't let much bother you, do you?"

"Uh . . . I don't know," I said.

"It's just that, you're always getting yourself into these crazy situations, but you never seem to lose it. You laughed off Mrs. Everly's matching outfit, you were in total control during the whole locker thing"—I cringed—"and now The Ball. I mean, if it were me, I would have transferred schools a long time ago."

"I would have left the school *district*," Kayla added.

Then they both started laughing. But you know what? It wasn't one of those laughing-at-you laughs; it was a laughing-with-you laugh. Even though I wasn't laughing, yet.

I said, "Yeah, so how about that announcement from Mr. Moran?"

"I couldn't believe it," Kayla said. "That was the longest three minutes of my life."

"Of *your* life?" I asked. "How do you think it was for me? At one point, I actually thought time wasn't moving at all."

"Oh, you poor thing!" Rosemary said. "We all felt so sorry for you after that stupid thing. I mean, could Mr. Moran have been any more over the top?"

"With the way things have been going for me," I said, "I think three minutes is right on par. Lately it's like I've been a complete glutton for punishment."

Rosemary laughed. "More like addicted to it," she said.

I'd had a library date with Jason, he'd invited me to his party, he talked to me in the halls, and now I stood with Rosemary and Kayla, talking and laughing. I was so close to my goal that I knew Jason's party would be the final performance I needed to get these people to nominate me.

Our school loves to keep the classrooms so ice cold that I always think I'm one degree away from hypothermia. I used to think they kept rooms like this because Texas is so hot, but Elisabeth once told me they do it to keep us from falling asleep in class. Which didn't make much sense when you consider that sometimes people freeze to death because they fall asleep in the snow, but whatever.

I sat in algebra shivering, goose bumps covering my entire

body. I kept my arms folded safely across the front of my thin T-shirt.

"Thurman!" Shiner whispered from across the aisle. Since the night of the exploding Ball, we'd picked up the habit of giving shy hellos and smiles to each other in the halls. I had realized that Shiner had never done anything to me—just like Ellen had said, back on Valentine's Day. And since he'd been so nice to me at the game and after I blew up The Ball, I made sure to always give him the benefit of the doubt.

"What?"

"How'd you do on the exam?"

I shrugged. "Don't know yet."

Mrs. Everly was passing back the exam she had given us a couple of days earlier. That normally would have been cause to freak out in a huge way, but I had actually felt pretty good about it, thanks to Jason's help and the extra studying I did (academics, No. 6).

"What'd you get?" I asked Shiner.

"Seventy-six."

A true miracle for Shiner Camry. Last semester I would have assumed he had cheated, but that day, I was really proud of him. "Way to go," I said.

I looked at Jason, sitting across the room, talking quietly with Richie Adams. We'd played it casual since the library sorta-date. Sometimes he walked with me out of English before he made his way across the courtyard. Aside from that, we hadn't talked much, and I worried that I was taking a backward step in my goal. I needed him to notice me—I needed them all to notice me. Jason sat with Richie, Rosemary, and the others at lunch, and I still sat with Kirstie, who kept threatening to invite Jason over to our table, saying I'd never get nominated if I didn't make a bold move, and soon.

"And I don't mean by exploding things," she had said. "Just remind yourself that you're a perfect match for a guy like Jason, and he'd be lucky to get a girl like you."

"A perfect match? How do you figure?"

"Please!" she huffed. "He used to be just like you are now, and so he can probably empathize with your current situation."

"You mean feel sorry for me?"

"*And,*" she continued, "you're very pretty *and* you never, ever give up."

"That last one I'll agree with." *For better or worse,* I silently added.

I snapped back to attention when I realized that Richie saw me looking at Jason. I quickly darted my eyes away. Right then, Mrs. Everly placed my quiz facedown on my desk, which could only mean one thing: a failing grade.

✳✳✳

"Sara! Wait up!"

Jason limped as fast as his walking cast would let him through the doors of algebra. I stopped in the middle of the crowded hall to wait for him, happy little butterflies zipping around my stomach—he hadn't forgotten about me after all.

"Hey," I said.

"So, how'd you do?"

"You first. What'd you get?"

"Ninety-six."

"Dang! Really?" I asked, happy he did so well.

"Okay, now you."

I pulled my crinkled quiz out of my bag and held it up for his inspection.

"Ninety-two? Hey, nice job, Thurman."

"Only the best I've done all semester," I said proudly as we headed down the hallway together past kids slamming their blue lockers shut.

"We make a pretty good team," he said, nudging me with his shoulder. I smiled and tucked my chin to my chest. "I go this way," he said, nodding in the opposite direction. "Will you be at basketball practice today?"

"Yeah. The guys are running court sprints," I said. "I gotta write the times."

"I'll be there, sitting on the bench. Maybe I can help you with the times."

I smiled at the image of Jason and me working together on stats. Between algebra, stats, and the upcoming party, we might be nominated Best Twosome in addition to Class Favorites.

"Cool," I said before watching him walk away.

After school I sat on a bench outside the gym to change into my tennis shoes. As I stuffed my Mary Janes into my messenger bag, I saw Arlene and Ellen Spitz coming toward me, chatting away like best buds. Arlene wore dark blue jeans and a top I knew she got in San Antonio two summers ago. It was white with embroidered flowers around the neckline. It was her favorite spring blouse even though it was girlie. I watched, feeling a new level of guilt and sadness at the way things had turned out for us.

I quickly jammed my books and folders into my bag. "Hey, Arlene," I called. I knew this would be hard, but I had to do it. I started to think that if I'd just spoken to her right when I'd felt that something wasn't right, then none of this would have happened. "Can I talk to you?"

Arlene told Ellen that she'd see her later, and Ellen gave me a look before she walked off that was a little like one of those given by publicists you see on red carpet events, ferociously protecting their star. I didn't like it.

"What?" Her curtness shouldn't have surprised me, but it did. I knew clearing the air with Arlene would be one of the hardest things I'd ever done, but I also knew that continuing to do nothing at all was even worse. Still, it was hard to know where to start.

Of course, being me, I said the absolute worst thing.

"Why do you hang with Ellen Spitz? She's kind of a hick."

Arlene's mouth dropped a little. "I hang out with her because she's *nice*."

I shook my head, angry at myself for saying that. The truth was, I was still jealous of Ellen—jealous that she was Arlene's best friend and I wasn't. Even though I had Kirstie as a friend, I guess I just felt territorial of Arlene "Look, Arlene, I didn't mean—"

"You know, Sara," Arlene interrupted, her tone surprisingly firm. "You think you're so great now that you're hanging out with Jason Andersen and that Kirstie girl. I hang out with Ellen because she's a good friend. She believes me when I tell her something."

"I know," I said, incredibly flustered. "You're right." I wasn't used to fighting with Arlene, and it looked like this could turn into our second fight since we had become friends. I didn't want that. I wasn't sure how to handle it, and I started to forget why I'd called her over in the first place. To ask her if she was the culprit of my locker? To tell her I was sorry I'd let things get so far gone? Or to say that, even if she had leaked word about the roses, that I forgave her? "Listen, I don't want to fight with you. I'm—"

"Do you ever think things through," she interrupted, "or do you always have to assume the worst? Like about the roses?"

"Look, all I know is," I said, feeling defensive, "you were the only one who knew who had sent them to me, and then suddenly the whole school knew."

"You know, Sara." Arlene shook her head. "Maybe all this started for you on the day your mom sent you those roses, but think real hard about what else happened that day."

When I realized she wasn't going to tell me, I snapped, *"What?"*

"Your new best friend Kirstie Luegner came to Bowie. Did you even read the e-mail I sent you? She was the only other person in the office that day. Have you even questioned if she was the one who spread the word?"

"Yeah, for your information, I did think about that," I said. "I know she didn't do it. I think you're just mad that Kirstie and I became friends and you weren't in on it. You've never liked her, and for no good reason."

"Maybe I have a reason." Arlene glared at me a moment, her face pale. When I didn't say anything, she said, "So I guess that's it, then. I guess we're really not friends anymore. Thanks for being so mature, Sara."

She stormed down the sidewalk, past the trees, until I couldn't see her anymore, and I knew that she was crying before she started running.

I wanted to cry too. I didn't know why this had to happen to us, especially since we'd been friends for so long. Was it some sort of woman's intuition that told me she was guilty? I didn't like how she was accusing Kirstie, who had never done anything to her. Why would Kirstie, the new girl, want to do that to someone she had just met? It all seemed so impossible.

♥ 17 ♥

Are You a Stand-up Stephanie or
a Push-over Penelope?

You have a huge term paper due tomorrow. Your best friend, Alexis, calls and begs you to go with her to the mall, where she knows her ex-boyfriend will be hanging out with his new girl. After she swears she'll never ask for another favor again, you:

a) agree only after she starts crying and asking how you can be so mean to someone you call "friend."

b) agree only if she buys you dinner at Wok 'N Roll.

c) tell her that you love her, but you have much more important things to do—and so should she.

Thinking about Arlene made my stomach cramp up. Suddenly I understood the expression "You look like you just lost your best friend." Kirstie had said that to me the day I got the roses, but now I felt it wholeheartedly. All during basketball practice, as I wrote down times and shots, I was in a daze.

Even with Jason only a few feet from me during practice, sitting on the bench watching plays and commenting with Coach Eckels, Arlene was the only thing I could think about. Except that one time Jason gave me a mischievous little wink and my heart went *pitter-patter-putter*, but other than that, it was all Arlene, all the time. After practice, as I walked past Jim's Grocery, the tiny little store that was our neighborhood's 7-Eleven, I thought sadly of all the Tangy Taffy and Orangina Arlene and I had bought there over the years for Razzie movie viewings and wondered if we'd ever stuff our faces with our favorite candy while watching bad movies again.

When I walked across our front yard, I noticed the Texas flag dangling from its enormous pole. It had been there ever since Dad put it up, and I wondered who would take it down if it rained. I pushed through the door, hoping for a quiet evening. I thought I might even do some homework.

"Any messages?" I asked Mom as she set iced tea on the table. She scooted around the linoleum floor in her black stockings, still wearing her clothes from the bank.

"No, sorry, honey," she said, pausing to untuck my hair from behind my ear. "You expecting a call?"

"Not really." I tucked my hair back.

"How was practice?" she asked, pulling plates down from

the cabinet. Since I had killed The Ball she had made a point to ask about my day.

"Fine." I shrugged.

"How are you?"

"Fine."

"Are you feeling okay? You've seemed so quiet lately."

"I'm fine."

"If you can think of another word other than *fine*, I'll give you five dollars." When I managed a smile, she sat down next to me. "You've just seemed so down lately. I'm worried. I haven't seen Arlene here in so long."

A part of me appreciated her making the effort, but it was just too hard to even think about, much less talk about. Then again, maybe part of being a mature woman was learning to deal with difficult stuff. Maybe by keeping mum, I was being immature? I wondered if that's what Mom and Dad did—avoided talking about the hard stuff until, eventually, they couldn't get back to the good stuff. We sat for a moment as I tried to gear up to actually talk about Arlene. I finally said, "Remember how someone trashed my locker?"

"Oh, honey." Even she seemed to wince at the visual. "I should have listened to you more when you were trying to tell me about that before spring break. I'm sorry."

"It's okay," I said. "Anyway, it's possible that it was Arlene who did that to me. We got in a fight—a couple, actually—and she hasn't admitted she did anything, but I'm still unsure. She's the only one I told about why you sent those roses on Valentine's Day, and word got out, anyway. I just don't know what to think anymore."

Mom said, "When best friends grow up together, sometimes, at some point, they do start to go in different directions. It's one of the worst realities of growing up—knowing that sometimes you drift apart. But I have to say, that as long as I've known Arlene, I've never known her to have a vindictive bone in her body. Doing something as cruel as defiling your locker just doesn't sound like something she'd do. Does it to you?"

It was a pretty simple question, with a pretty simple answer. "No," I said. "But how do I know for sure?"

"Sometimes," Mom said, "you just have to have blind faith. If you believe Arlene didn't do it, then she didn't do it. It can be as simple as that."

Simple, but not really. I needed to think on it some more. "Thanks, Mom," I said. "And I'm sorry I got so mad at you about those flowers. It really was a nice gesture, and I'm sorry I acted like such a brat."

She smoothed down the back of my hair and said, "It's okay."

After dinner that night, I lay on my bed, staring at the ceiling, listening to KPOP and trying to feel good about something, anything. I ran over every single thing Arlene and I had said that afternoon, mentally marking places where I should have said or done something differently. I even thought about Kirstie, and Arlene's attack on her. Kirstie had said that she was Most Popular at her last school, but here in Ladel, I was still her only friend.

My stomach became one big pretzel knot. Talking to Mom had made me feel a little better, but the dinner she had cooked didn't do my stomach any favors. She had made chipped beef with white bread and peas—a meal so disgusting, I had a hard time believing anyone actually liked it.

Still, she was right: The locker thing didn't seem like something Arlene would do. Things weren't too far gone to get them back, if it was important enough. I *was* being immature about the whole thing, and although I didn't know who had leaked word about the period roses or who "decorated" my locker, I should have listened to Arlene instead of jumping to my own conclusions. I started to wonder if I'd even given her a chance.

I got up and strolled down the hall to the computer.

I had one new e-mail.

My heart leaped with hope while my head told me it was probably junk mail—a subscription reminder from one of my magazines, a forwarded story from some distant relative, or, better yet, a virus. That would make my life even more perfect.

I clicked on my in box and read: Kirstie Luegner.

Hey! What's up. I'm so bored. If you finish your science, call me. I'm so not in the mood to do it tonight.
Anyway, heard about Jason's party Saturday p.m. You must be so excited! But what will you wear???? Plz no more Mrs. Everly-inspired outfits!! We could go over together, if you want. Wanna get dressed at my house? You can borrow anything you want. We could discuss CF-strategies: clothes, conversation (what WILL you talk about??) and attitude!!
Gotta go. Call me!
XO.

The party was just what I needed—something to take the edge off. The what-to-wear dilemma alone could occupy me for days. Focusing on the party as my final step in wooing the eighth-grade class of Bowie Junior High into voting for me for Class Favorite was just the distraction I needed.

From: Sara Thurman
To: Kirstie Luegner
Subject: Re: SATURDAY!!!

Hey! I'm trying to get into my science HW but haven't made it past filling in the blank where it asks Name. :) I'll probably finish it on the way to school tomorrow, but if I get it done before then, I'll call u. Have you started it at all?

Yes, let's definitely get dressed at your house on Saturday. I'm VERY excited about the party!!!!!!!!! This will be like my Academy Awards night, it's that important.

I know it's going to be so much fun. I'm gonna go thru my closet right now and c what I have to wear. It has to be awesome. Suggestions?

C ya tomorrow.

Sara

While I waited for her to write me back, I thought about the clothes situation for the party. Should I wear a skirt, a dress, jeans? Sneakers, heels, boots? A low-cut shirt or a belly shirt? I reminded myself that Jason's party would be my red carpet, Haden Prescott moment. I had to look and act sophisticated, mature, and gracious.

I stared at the monitor, clicking the refresh button obsessively. Really, I was just avoiding writing or calling Arlene. I knew I should do it, but something held me back—fear of the truth, and what that might mean for us? Maybe just the fear of the fight. This may sound like an obvious statement, but

I hated fighting with Arlene. It was such an unnatural, scary feeling. I guess by calling her, I feared I might learn a truth about her I'd never be ready to hear.

So, I distracted myself with my magazines. I picked one up off the floor and started flipping. All of "Summer's Saucy Skirts and Shirts" were either too trendy for me to pull off or too expensive. Then I tested my "Fashion IQ" and scored in the "Seriously Slacking" category. It suggested I "explore a little place most towns have, called The Mall. You might even find some great friends there who can help transform you from a Slacker Sister to the Goddess of Your Grade!" I tossed the magazine aside. I considered DIY-ing my Mrs. Everly skirt but decided I didn't have the creative energy. I sighed and clicked refresh again. I wondered if I was over-thinking the clothes thing. The key to the party was more than my outward appearance, after all, just as Haden Prescott was more than her golden Oscar gown.

Back in my room I dug up another magazine from the edge of my closet and searched for something more mind-oriented. There was a yoga section that promised to ease the mind and soothe the body—exactly what I needed. I attempted to strike a one-arm balance.

When I finally steadied myself, my arm shaking to hold up my weight, my door flew open; when I looked up, I fell forward onto my stomach, smashing my face in the carpet.

"What was *that*?" Elisabeth stood with an amused and confused look on her tanned face.

"Don't you knock?"

"No."

"What do you want?"

"It's your night to do the dishes."

"I'll do them later. Now get out."

"I need a favor," she said, plopping down on my bed.

"Don't get sweat all over my sheets," I said, looking her over. "What do you want?"

"Since you have no life, it's really no big deal. I need you to babysit the Medina twins Saturday night."

"Forget it," I said adamantly. "I have plans, for your information."

"Too bad." She tightened her ponytail. "I'm running regionals that night. It's a big deal that you wouldn't understand, and I'm not going to miss it. Even Mom said so."

"She did not," I snapped. "Why would Mom agree? Besides, those kids hate me. The one and only time I sat for them, they locked me in the closet."

Elisabeth gave a little chuckle at this.

"Shut up," I told her, crossing my arms over my chest.

"Remember that time," she began, gazing up at the ceiling, "I saved your butt by getting Coach Eckels to make you a stat girl?" She was so pleased with herself, she looked like she was about to pop right out of her sports bra. "Payback time."

"No way," I said, standing up. "For your information, I have *plans* Saturday night, and I'm not about to break them. No freakin' way. Uh-uh. Forget it." I propped my hands on my hips and stood defiantly. I hadn't come all this way just to let my evil sister get petty over a favor owed. Plus, those twins were little monsters. I hated them as much as they hated me.

Elisabeth nodded her head and stayed annoyingly calm. And then:

"Mom!" she screamed, standing up from my bed and walking to the door. "Mom! Sara's going back on a promise!" This was definitely not good. Every time Elisabeth brought Mom into our fights, she always came out on top.

"Are you kidding? Mom's not going to *make* me babysit. She can't make me!"

"What's this yelling about?" Mom said when she appeared in the doorway. "You know I don't like yelling in my house."

"Mother, Sara made a promise to me and now she's going back on it. I need her to babysit for me Saturday night so I can run at regionals. Coach will be pissed—"

"Watch your mouth," Mom warned.

"—and now Sara won't help me out," Elisabeth finished.

"But I have plans!" I said. "Mom, I can't. I'm going to a party at the *Andersens'*."

"Big deal," Elisabeth snipped. "Oooh, the *Andersens'*."

"Shut up!"

"Mom! She told me to shut up!"

"All right, enough, both of you!" Mom snapped. "I said I don't want yelling in my house. Sara, don't talk to your sister like that."

"But, Mom—"

"Sara." She rubbed her hand across her forehead as if a headache were coming on. I knew it just meant she didn't know how to handle the situation. There was still hope. "Elisabeth, tell me what's going on."

"Fine. A few weeks ago Sara wanted me to get her the position as Coach Eckels's stat girl—which I did—and she promised to do anything I asked."

"I didn't say I'd do *anything*!"

"Sara!" Mom said, her eyes closed before letting out a big breath. "Let your sister finish."

"Anyway," Elisabeth huffed. "She said she'd return the favor when I asked her. And now I'm asking her. I told the Medinas I'd babysit for them and then found out about the track thing. It's usually on Saturday afternoon, but they had scheduling problems, so we're running at night. Mom, you know I can't miss it. It'll totally mess up my record and all this work I've been doing."

Mom sighed and said, "I know, honey."

"Can I talk now?" I asked before they really started bonding over how much of a star Elisabeth was.

"Did you promise you'd help your sister out?" Mom asked.

"Well, yes, ma'am, but I didn't say I'd do *any* thing, *any* time. Mom, I have plans. It's not fair. I could do it any other night but this night. Besides, we're not the only babysitters in town. They can find someone else."

"They like us," Elisabeth hissed.

"They like *you*."

"Girls, please." She thought for a moment, then said, "You know I don't like you going back on promises. That includes you," she said to Elisabeth, "backing out of your obligation to the Medinas."

"But there's nothing I can do," she pleaded.

She turned to me and said, "Sara, you haven't even asked me if you could go to this party. I don't know anything about it. Will Jason's parents be there? Who else is going? You haven't told me anything. . . ."

"I just found out about it!" I tried.

"That's not the point. You know the rules about parties. And you can't just decide to go out to a party without asking permission. I'd want to talk to his mother beforehand."

"How was I supposed to know you had this rule if I've never been to parties except for Arlene's?" I cried. Elisabeth smirked at that, but I almost didn't care—that's how desperate I was.

Mom turned her back to Elisabeth and looked me in the eyes. "Sara, honey. What do you think we should do?"

"I don't know! She already said she'd babysit!" I knew I was losing control, but it was too hard to pull myself back.

Mom said, "Sara. I'm asking you again. What do you think we should do?"

I realized this was a moment, a lesson my mom was trying to teach me. I was going to have to play along. I thought for a moment—telling Elisabeth to miss regionals wasn't the answer; neither was my giving in and missing Jason's party. "There are other babysitters around," I said. "Maybe I can call the Medinas, tell them what's going on, and tell them I'm going to call around for other sitters if it's okay with them."

Mom nodded. "That's a good idea. Maybe they have someone they can call on too."

"Good luck with that," Elisabeth piped in. "They never go out, and when they do, it's me they call."

"Thank you, Elisabeth." Mom sighed. She looked back to me and said, "If you give me the number to the Andersens', I'll call about the party. If everything is in order, then you can go. But only on the condition that you find a replacement for the Medinas that's to their satisfaction. If not, then you need to do this favor for your sister."

I couldn't believe she was choosing *now* to teach me some

life lesson. The party was too important to me. Still, there was hope, and it was all in my hands.

As I stood in my room, looking at the two of them—my own flesh and blood, the only people in the world besides Dad who were legally obligated to like me—I felt like they were against me. "Well, can you at least tell Elisabeth to stop smirking at me?" She looked like she'd just won the Universe Cup or something, she was looking so pleased with herself.

"Elisabeth," Mom said wearily. "Behave yourself."

"And get out of my room while you're at it," I added, giving her a little shove.

"Mom!" Elisabeth whined.

"Sara, I said that's enough. Now I suggest you get to work on this."

Before they shut my door, Elisabeth turned back, smiling, and said, "And don't forget: It's your night to do the dishes."

I stood staring at the closed door and squared my shoulders. It was up to me to get myself out of this mess. I decided to call the Medinas first—maybe they knew of another neighborhood kid who could cover for me. I decided to be up front and honest with them about the whole situation, since honesty was supposed to be the best policy.

"Normally we'd ask our niece," Mrs. Medina said. "But she's got a track meet. Sounds like it's the same one as Elisabeth's."

"Oh," I said.

"So you will be here on Saturday, right?"

"I promise, someone will be there. Don't worry."

I picked up my Bowie Junior High phone directory and started flipping through the names, trying to figure out who I could call without it seeming totally random. With my heart pounding, I called a girl from my gym class named Heidi who I knew loved kids because she always talked about what she was going to name her future children (Michael, Samantha, and Lola, in that order).

"What's your name again?" she asked. When I told her, she said, "Oh! The girl who blew up The Ball!"

I had the exact same conversation with three other girls, but all of them had other plans. I thought of taking an ad out in the Ladel *Pennysaver*, but it was an outrageous idea, and besides, there wasn't enough time to do it before Saturday. There was only one person left who I could call, and I couldn't call her asking for a favor. If I called Arlene at all, it had to be to talk things out. And that was still one call I was avoiding.

Later, after I'd slaved over the dishes (that chipped beef sauce was especially hard to scrape off), I slumped back to my room. I closed my closet door and stacked my magazines on the corner of my desk and tucked my CF list into my desk drawer. I no longer needed to worry about finding the right clothes and attitude for the party. There would be no great conversations with Jason, no giggling with Rosemary. Come Monday morning I'd still be a nobody, some girl in their class, the one who blew up The Ball that one time. I stared at the Class Favorite pictures I had taped up beside the pictures of Haden Prescott triumphing on the Oscars red carpet. I looked down at my hands and thought of the events of the last few weeks and, before I could tell myself to stop feeling sorry for myself, I started to cry.

♥18♥

Are You Really Best Friends Forever?

True or False: I know that I can trust my best friend with anything I tell her.

The morning of the party I stayed in bed until 11:30, and the only reason I got up at all was because there was a phone call for me.

"Are you so excited about tonight you're ready to vomit?" Kirstie asked. I could hear a blender in the background and wondered what she was mixing. Smoothies? I had seriously thought of just not showing up at the Medinas, but in the end I decided that I couldn't do that. It was a way too mean thing to do.

"No," I said flatly. "I'm miserable. I'm not going."

"What, got cold feet? Sara, it's just a party."

I sat up in bed, pulled the comforter up to my waist, and realized my eyes were swollen from crying. "Seriously, Kirstie. I can't go."

"Did you get grounded again?" she asked. I could now hear a television in the background. She must have moved rooms, and I had an image of her sitting on the puffy off-white couch, flipping through the channels as I told her my latest heart-crushing moment.

"No. I have to babysit for my sister. She has some stupid track thing tonight, and I have to cover."

"Wait a minute," she started. "How can you not be going to the one thing you've been waiting forever to go to?"

"I haven't been waiting forever to go to his party."

"But you've been drooling over this guy since, what, puberty?"

I wanted to bury myself at the reminder of anything related to my period. "I know," I said miserably.

"But tonight could be your *Silent Widow*," she miserably said, referring to Haden Prescott's Academy Award–nominated role. "How old are the little monsters, anyway?"

"Six." I slid back under the covers.

"At least there's just one."

"No, they're *both* six."

"What, twins? Oh man, that totally sucks, Sara."

"Thanks. I know," I moaned.

"Well," she said, taking a gulp of something. The smoothie? "Do you mind if I still go?"

"No," I said. "Of course not."

"Cool. I've actually been looking forward to it. Make some new friends and all."

I swallowed, wondering if she was already over me. She acted so self-assured, talking about showing up at a party by herself— something I'd never do. Kirstie was cute, nice, and bold at times, and I wondered again why a former Most Popular hadn't made more friends at our school. Maybe I was toxic?

"Want me to give Jason a message or anything? A big fat sloppy kiss from you?" When I didn't say anything, Kirstie said, "Kidding! Sara, I was totally kidding."

To say that the thought of Kirstie taking my much-dreamed-of night with Jason for herself made me nauseated would be the biggest understatement in the history of human-kind. When I got off the phone with her, I lay in bed a while longer, staring across the room.

I wondered if I should call Jason or maybe e-mail him to tell him I wasn't coming. Then again, it wasn't like he was having the party for me. If I didn't show up, no one would even notice. No one understood the importance of this party. I really liked Jason—he was sweet and totally cute and he seemed to genuinely like me. I thought the party would take us to the next level. Not to mention all the work I'd done on my CF goal and how close I was to getting people to like me for more than making a fool of myself. Now, I thought, come Monday morning, everything would just be the same.

I managed to drag myself out of bed, pull on a pair of almost-clean socks I found in the corner by my desk and barbeque-stained jeans from the back of my chair, and wiped the sleep out of my eyes in lieu of washing my face. Today, I would do the minimum of everything.

The house was quiet. I peeked in Elisabeth's room on my way to the kitchen and saw that her bed was made and she was nowhere in sight. She was probably out running. Elisabeth ran even on the days she ran. I wondered if she ever got frustrated that, despite all that running and all that distance, the only place she ever got was back to where she had started. She was like a fish in a bowl—always in motion but never really getting anywhere.

In the kitchen I decided to make a peanut butter and jelly sandwich for my breakfast/lunch, then got lazy and decided on a simple peanut butter sandwich. I poured the last of the milk into a glass and ate standing at the counter. I thought about Jason and what could have been.

Mom's car pulled up outside, and when she came in carrying grocery bags, she asked, "Did you just get up?"

"No," I lied.

"Why don't you put on some cleaner clothes?" She rested the bags on the counter near my milk and dropped her keys and purse beside them.

"I don't know. I will."

Mom rested her hand on the counter and gave me her worried look. "Oh, honey," she began. "I'm sorry about the party. I know it doesn't seem fair, and I know it seems like there won't be any other parties, but trust me: There will be. Running is important to Elisabeth—it could mean a college scholarship for her in a couple of years. There are worse things that could happen than not being able to go to one party."

"Mom, I *know*." How could I explain to her that this wasn't just one party—it was *the* party? "But that doesn't make me feel better, okay? Look, I don't even care anymore. I'm baby-sitting, and that's that. I can use the money, anyway."

"At least you did everything you could to remedy the situation, right?"

"I guess."

I took my sandwich and milk and sat at the table. It was sunny out, and the trees were waving at me in their light breeze. *A perfect day for a party,* I thought miserably.

"Oh, shoot," Mom said, looking in the fridge. "I didn't realize we were out of milk." She gave a huge sigh, like this was the worst that could happen. Talk about not listening to your own advice.

She turned her attention to me and, apparently noticing again how I had obviously just rolled out of bed, said, "Run to Jim's for me and get some, will you?" She dug some money out of her purse and handed it over to me. "You look like you could use a nice walk. It's beautiful out, you know." She smiled at me in a way that made me not want to argue. She was trying so hard.

It *was* pretty out. It was cool enough for jeans but warm enough for short sleeves, and the air was somehow weighted with the promise of the hot summer to come. The walk to Jim's Grocery took about ten minutes, down our street, across Reagan Park to Oak Hill Drive, where one of the volleyball coaches lived, and on to Spring Creek Avenue. Ladel doesn't have many sidewalks, except in nice neighborhoods and maybe in what passes for our downtown, so I had to walk on the strip of gravel and weeds between the road and the ditch. Mom used to always tell to us to walk with traffic, but Dad told us to walk against it so that we could see the cars coming. I walked against it.

Jim was from Vietnam and of an indefinite age—he somehow looked old, but didn't have any wrinkles. He could have been twenty or ninety, I had no idea. His store had been robbed twice—both times at gunpoint—but for some reason the neighborhood was still considered a good one, proven by the fact that Mom let me walk there by myself.

"Hi!" Jim said enthusiastically when I walked through the chiming door, and I smiled back at him. Mom had given me plenty of money for the milk, so I decided to buy some candy for the walk back.

The candy aisle was directly in Jim's view from the cash register, I guess to keep an eye on kids who thought about stealing. When I turned into the aisle from the side of the store, I stopped dead, almost knocking over the Pringles display: Arlene was there, three Tangy Taffy bars in one hand, looking at the rest of her options. I took a step back, hiding behind the single-serving Pringles cans.

She was wearing cut-off sweatpants and an oversize T-shirt, and her hair was tangled and pulled back into a sloppy ponytail. She looked about as happy to be alive as I felt. I watched her reach down to the bottom rack for a Cherry Mash—two of them—before it hit me. More like smacked me full-on upside my head. It was *our* night to watch Raspberry Award movies. I had been so completely focused on Jason and making my way toward the Class Favorite ballot that our tradition had slipped from my mind for the first time since we'd started it. And there she was, going through the motions of our ritual alone.

I assumed she would turn toward the back where the drinks were, but she turned the other way—my way—and suddenly we were standing face-to-face. I felt like I'd been caught spying. I guess I had been.

"Oh," Arlene said, stopping abruptly in front of me. I took a little step back, wishing I hadn't lingered. "I didn't see you there," she said, shifting the candy awkwardly in her hands.

She waited, almost expectantly, though she wouldn't look

at me. She didn't look angry, and for that, I was grateful. I didn't know what to say. I didn't want to ignore her or fight with her or insult her. I wanted to burst out, "I'm sorry!" and give her a big tight hug, even though we weren't the hugging type. Seeing her at Jim's, her fists filled with our favorite candy, obviously preparing for a Saturday night alone, made me want to drop everything and just be with her.

I scratched at the single-serving Pringles cans nervously, and when she realized I wasn't going to talk, Arlene said, "So. I guess you're going to Jason's big party tonight." Her voice was stiff and strained, as if getting the words out were a major chore. I could tell she wanted to be tough with me, but I heard the hesitation in her voice. "I heard some people talking about it in the halls. Y'all a couple now?"

"I don't know," I muttered, still not looking at her. It seemed like an odd question, in light of what had happened between us. I wanted us—Arlene and I—to be friends again. But it's hard to just come right out and say that, especially when there was a lingering doubt of loyalty.

"Well," Arlene prompted again, taking control of the conversation like I should have done. "I guess you have a lot of exfoliating to do. Or something." There was no hesitation in her voice now—it was full of edge and anger. She turned her back to me and walked to the cooler, swiftly grabbing a large bottle of Orangina. "So have fun," she added sarcastically.

"I'm not going," I bleated. "I have to babysit the Medina twins. It's this whole stupid thing with my sister. She has some running thing, and I called everyone I know"—*except you!* I wanted to say—"but no one can do it, so I have to miss the party." I took a breath and let out a big sigh, and was amazed that I felt slightly calm.

"Well," Arlene began cautiously, her voice softening as she shifted the goodies in her arms. "I can't say that you don't deserve it."

"Forget it," I said quickly. The last thing I wanted was to hear her say *I told you so.* I started to leave, upset I had told her about babysitting.

"Look, wait a sec."

I turned to face her, but only looked at her for a second. In a lightning glance, she looked annoyed.

"I can't believe I'm about to do this," she mumbled. She closed her eyes and inhaled. "I know how much you like Jason—I've watched you drool over him all year. I'm sure this party is a huge deal for you, so if you want, I'll watch the Medinas for you tonight."

I think *gobsmacked* would be the best word to describe my reaction. *As in, Wait a second, did I just hear what I think I heard?* And then, *Is this a trick?*

"I've sat for the twins before," Arlene continued. "They like me. I'm sure their parents won't mind."

I just stood there, completely silent, unable to blink or close my gaping mouth.

After a long pause, she said, "So, anyway, I'll call Mrs. Medina and make sure it's okay and get the details. I guess I'll call you if there's a problem. Otherwise," she said, heading toward Jim's counter, "have fun with Jason."

"No, you don't have to," I finally managed.

"It's fine," she said, handing her money over to Jim.

I felt like grabbing her from behind and giving her a huge hug. It wasn't just that she was making it possible for me to go to Jason's party—it was more than that. She was doing something so selfless, especially considering all that had happened to us in the last couple of months. I didn't deserve her. I was the world's worst person getting a mark of kindness from the Goddess of Nice. In those moments, I realized all that I was losing when I didn't have a friend like Arlene in my life.

She took her sack of candy from Jim and started toward the door.

"Arlene, wait!" I called. She turned back to me. There were so many things I wanted to say to her, so much to get out. But all I could manage was the simplest of words: "Thank you."

For a moment, she looked like she wanted to smile at me. She didn't, but she did say, "You're welcome," before heading out the door.

♥19♥

Do You Know How to Party?

Your swim team just had its third victory in a row, so you invite the team over on Saturday night to celebrate. The vibe is:

a) raucous—come as you are, bring who you please, and turn the noise up!

b) low-key—only the girls on the team are invited for a movie-watching marathon complete with tons of junk food.

c) elegant—below-the-knee skirts are a must at the three-course dinner you're catering.

As I walked home from Jim's Grocery, I found myself in a daze. I was so completely dumbfounded, baffled, and shocked by what had just happened with Arlene that I walked with traffic instead of against it.

My mind was all over the place. Why would Arlene do that? Was it her way of apologizing to me? Was she just feeling guilty about (possibly) sabotaging my life, or was it possible that I had been wrong all along, that she didn't tell anyone about the roses or have anything to do with my locker, and this was her way of showing me that she'd always be my friend, no matter what *I* did?

Or . . . was it another plot to ruin me? Maybe she told me she would babysit the Medinas but had no intention of ever showing up. I'd still get in huge trouble, Mom would ground me until I graduated from college, and Jason and I would never have a chance to fall in love.

But then I tossed my suspicions in the ditch. I was more confused than ever, but I had to remember that this was the girl who was the only one there for me when my folks split up. Okay, so she did tell some of her friends about my parents' split, but I hadn't exactly told her *not* to. I couldn't ignore the fact that she made that entire weekend in December All About Sara Weekend. She told me we could do anything I wanted, that we could even go to Six Flags despite the fact that it was freezing and they were doing the Holiday in the Park thing, which is lame but we love it. But all I wanted to do was watch as many movies as we could stand, so Arlene's mom checked out four from the video store; after we watched them, she returned them and checked out four more for the next day. My eyes were killing me by the end of the weekend from staring at the TV for so long, but it was awesome because it had really gotten my mind off all the stuff that was happening at home. After that weekend I had counted myself lucky to have such a great best friend.

How could I be expected to have fun at the party knowing Arlene was working her butt off trying to control those two screaming brats? And that once she put them in bed, she'd watch a really horrible movie alone? I'd tried watching *Catwoman* alone over spring break, and it only made me more depressed. When I watched bad movies alone, I realized they were no longer so bad, they were good—they were just bad. And knowing that Arlene would suffer through that while I was off being charming with Bowie's hottest guy made me feel like dirt.

Should I skip the party and go to the Medinas with Arlene?

As I pushed through the screen door of our house, I knew the answer. I mean, who was I kidding? Despite my suspicions, Arlene was over-the-top in her niceness, and maybe I was being totally selfish, but still—it was Jason. The decision made me fully depressed, but in a way, I thought, *I'm doing it for Arlene, too.* You know, having enough fun for both of us. Anyway, it helped me feel one molecule better.

When Kirstie opened her door, the smell of vanilla attacked my nostrils. It was sickly sweet, and when I stepped inside, I had to rub my nose to ward off a sneeze attack.

"Can you believe it?" I said, kicking off my shoes by the door. "It's like I got a temporary reprieve or something." I pulled my bag up over my shoulder—I didn't know what to wear, so I basically had brought everything—and followed Kirstie up the stairs to her room.

"I can't believe Arlene did that," Kirstie said. I had called her as soon as I got home and told her the whole thing. "Do you think it's because she feels guilty?"

"Not at all. We didn't talk about all the stuff that's happened, but I have to tell you, I don't think Arlene did it. Any of it. I'm going to talk to her—tomorrow, I think."

"Yeah, I would," Kirstie said. "Just to make sure."

"No, you don't understand. I *know* she's not responsible. It's just not in her nature. She's my best friend, and first thing tomorrow, I'm going to make it right."

"Wow." Kirstie laughed. "Well, don't let me stop you." For a moment she looked like she was going to say something more. But then she said, "Why don't you take a bath? It'll help you mellow out. My tub is huge, and I have the scrubs and bubbles and smell-good stuff. Help yourself to any of it."

So I did. The water was so hot, it made my skin red and my forehead sweat, but I didn't care. I was nervous about the night, but the warmth of the enormous tub made me feel like I was wrapped in a big, comforting blanket. I closed my eyes and fell into a deep almost-sleep.

Kirstie's shuffling around in her room snapped me out of a fantasy I was having about Jason that involved the sun setting on a lake and Cherry Sours. The water had turned lukewarm, and the bubbles were almost gone.

I quickly finished scrubbing and loofahing myself. When I came out, towel wrapped around me, Kirstie was shoving hangers aside in her closet

"The bath was awesome," I told her. "I feel all mushy and relaxed. Know what you're going to wear?"

"I have no idea. I have absolutely no clothes."

"Please," I said. "You have the cutest stuff." I picked up my bag and said, "Will you look at the stuff I brought and help me pick something out? Remember, this is like my Oscar night—I have to shine in every way."

"Is Haden Prescott your muse once again?" She picked up a couple of the things from my bag, then dropped them without interest.

"Actually, I feel sort of like I've done all I can to reach my goal—I need tonight to bring it all home. Think about it: I've worked tirelessly on my list. I talked to Rosemary and Kayla and they actually laughed *with* me, not *at* me. People are starting to see me as a normal human being. So tonight, I need to keep up with all I've already done. And I'm really going to work on the confidence thing. I'm trying to be more like that in life in general—not just for the Class Fave thing."

"Okay," Kirstie said. "But I want you to look beautiful on the outside. Cool?"

And so together we ransacked her closet until we found the perfect outfit for me: these great cranberry-colored pants with casual little ties at the bottom, two-inch strappy heels, and this totally cute form-fitting sleeveless shirt with a graphic from the 19-teens. It had a sailor girl on it and it read, GEE!! I WISH I WERE A MAN! I'D JOIN THE NAVY. It was from an actual recruitment poster from, like, World War I, and it was beyond retro.

"We've come a long way, baby!" I joked to Kirstie.

"Sara. Please." And I made a mental note to watch my nerdiness.

We finished the outfit off with a loose chain-link belt that rested casually on my hips. Everything I had on was Kirstie's—except my JCPenney underwear. I had picked out my sexiest, even though I knew Jason wouldn't see them. They were kind of babyish, with a little blue flower in the middle of the bra, but they had lace on them, which made me feel sort of grown up.

"Sara," Kirstie said, looking over the finished me, "you look awesome. That shirt is perfect for you." I checked myself out in the mirror again. "You should just keep it. It looks too good on you."

"Really? No, I can't keep it. It's yours."

"I'm telling you," she said, "you're hot in that shirt. How can I possibly ever wear it again knowing you could be wearing it?"

I could feel my face beaming with pleasure, and later, as we headed to her mom's car, the butterflies in my stomach could hardly contain themselves for the excitement of the night that was ahead. When her mom dropped us off, telling us to call her when we were ready, I stared at Jason's house, feeling as if I couldn't move from the spot on the sidewalk. His house was a little bigger than mine, but in a neighborhood with actual sidewalks, which somehow made it seem fancier. I took a deep breath and looked to Kirstie.

"Ain't nothin' but a party," she said. She flipped her thick black hair back over her shoulder, stood up a little straighter, and said, "So are you ready to do this or what?" She even gave me a little wink as we headed up the redbrick walk toward the front door of Jason Andersen's home.

Inside, I felt a sense of un-reality. I mean, there I was! I was standing in the home of the guy I'd been pining over for *so long*. Whether I was ready for it or not, it was really happening now. I had, in a sense, arrived.

Saying *everyone* was there sort of sounds cliché, but I'm sorry—it *did* seem like everyone was there. I could see Rosemary and Kayla in the kitchen, and Richie was in the living room, holding Mike Spencer in a playful headlock as the guys laughed and the girls pretended to ignore them. Also in the living room were a cluster of cheerleaders watching some football types play video games. Sprinkled throughout were student council members, more athletes, and even a few honor society people. I knew who most of the people were but doubted many knew who I was, unless they knew me as that girl who blew up The Ball . . . or that girl who got the period roses . . . or the girl who dresses like Mrs. Everly. . . .

"Oh, my gosh, Kirstie. Look at all these people. I don't even know this many people, much less have this many friends," I said, standing in the entryway next to Kirstie, taking in the scene. "I'm the biggest loser here," I added pathetically.

"Don't be stupid," Kirstie said, nudging me in the ribs. "You're the coolest one here."

I didn't believe that at all, but it was comforting hearing it. It gave me a little boost.

"I guess we should mingle or something?" I knew talking to Rosemary and Kayla was one of the first things I had to do, but I'd never mingled before and wasn't sure how to do it. Was it basically just butting into people's conversations, but in a nice way? I was grateful Kirstie was there with me, and I looked at her for reassurance. She shook her shiny hair back from her shoulders, cocked her chin up, and started walking as if she knew exactly where she was going. I tried to do the same.

We headed to the kitchen, where there was food, tons of it: guacamole and chips and salsa, cute little burritos the size of a roll of quarters, Cheetos, bowls of bite-size Snickers and Reese's, a steaming Crock-Pot of queso dip. Plus tons of drinks: punch, Coke, Diet Coke, Dr Pepper, iced tea . . . Orangina. I tried not to think of Arlene.

"I'm grabbing a drink," Kirstie said, searching out the faces. "You want something?"

I looked toward Rosemary and Kayla over by the guacamole and thought I'd better get on with it and make a social move. "A Diet Coke. I'm gonna get some chips."

Kirstie sauntered off toward the drinks as I tucked my hair behind my ear and headed to the girls. I had no idea what I was going to say to them, but I knew I wanted the night to go well on so many different levels. I didn't just want to woo Jason; I wanted to woo everyone.

I picked up a paper plate and napkin and moved in closer to them to eavesdrop a little, to try to find a way into their conversation.

"I think he likes her," Rosemary was saying. "Why else would he have said that?"

"Yeah, I guess." Kayla sighed.

I grabbed a handful of tortilla chips and picked up the spoon for the guac. "Oh, hey, y'all," I said, all casual-like, as if I'd spotted them by absolute chance. "How's it going?" I think

I sounded relatively calm, but my insides were completely flipping out. There was a moment of pause, the time between my last word and their first. Those moments were only milliseconds long, but they felt like a day. I waited eagerly, nervously, wondering what would happen next.

"Sara, hey," Rosemary said, popping a pretzel in her mouth. "Jason said you might come. What's up?"

"Hey," I answered, trying to act indifferent so they wouldn't know that I felt like screaming with excitement. He'd been talking about me?! "He invited me the other day. Actually, after I blew up The Ball." I snickered, remembering what a laugh that had brought the girls the other day. "I think he felt sorry for me."

Both girls smiled, and immediately I felt a hint of reassurance. After all, they were talking to me again. By Monday, there was no doubt that I'd be sitting with them at lunch. Coming to the party was really going to seal my fate.

"You poor thing," Kayla said. "Even though I'll probably never get tired of laughing about it, I still feel so horrible that you went through all that. I think it's cool that you did something that could never again be duplicated in the history of this school. It'll be one of those things where you'll always remember where you were and what you were wearing when it happened—like my granddaddy when Kennedy was shot."

"Remember how Sean Hurley's little sister started shaking and screaming and she couldn't move from her seat, she was so scared?" Rosemary reminisced.

"I know!" Kayla exclaimed. "I heard she peed her pants."

"God, not those cute little pink capris? They looked adorable on her."

"I know," Kayla said, shaking her head sadly. "But that's what I heard."

"Tell her to send me the dry-cleaning bill," I joked.

Rosemary and Kayla laughed, with Rosemary lightly touching my forearm as she did. I realized I was nodding in some sort of agreement and immediately stopped before they wondered if my head was coming loose from my neck.

"Speaking of cute clothes," Rosemary said, turning to me as I was shoveling a chip loaded with guacamole into my mouth, "I love that shirt."

"Totally," Kayla agreed through pretzel crunches. "I noticed it when you came in."

Rosemary pulled on the corner of the shirt, gently, to feel the fabric, I guess. It was just cotton. "Where did you get this?" she asked. "It's too cute."

I didn't want her to know it wasn't mine. I'm not sure why. I guess it made me cooler if I had picked it out and bought it myself. So I said, "Oh, I don't remember. Some shop in Dallas, I think."

"Well, it's adorable," Rosemary said. " 'Gee, I wish I were a man,' " she read. "Kayla, we should totally bring back the word *gee*, don't you think? It'd be so Jimmy Stewart."

Kayla looked to me with her eyebrows raised and said, "I don't think so." And then she laughed, and so did I.

"Shut up, y'all," Rosemary said.

"Gee, Rose," Kayla mocked. "Don't get so upset. Everything's going to be swell." And then we all laughed, and it was so completely wonderful that I was actually feeling comfortable and not all intimidated like I usually do.

Kirstie appeared beside me, bumping me with her hip, a red plastic cup in her hand, and said hello to the girls.

"It's Kirstie, right?" Kayla asked. "Rosemary and I were just telling Sara how cute she looks."

"I know," Kirstie said, eyeing me. "I think we got her packaged up and put together pretty nicely." I flinched at her words, but tried not to show it.

"Well," Rosemary began, "she looks great. I love her top."

"Thanks. I gave it to her," Kirstie said, taking a sip of her drink. Rosemary and Kayla looked from me to Kirstie. I smiled meekly.

Finally, Rosemary turned her attention to me and said, "Actually, Sara, Jason is so excited to see you tonight."

"Really?" I said.

"Yeah," she continued. "He keeps asking us if we've seen

you yet. I think he was worried you wouldn't come."

I smiled so wide, I had to look down at my chips to keep from showing so much of my excitement.

"Hello, ladies," said my most favorite voice in all the world. Jason leaned between Rosemary and Kayla, his arms resting around each girl's shoulders, which made them both smile instantly. I quickly wished I had been standing where they were. I glanced at Kirstie, who looked a little put off. "I must say, you are all looking quite lovely this evening. How's everyone doing?" He looked from girl to girl and only glanced at me—I think. I could barely bring myself to look at him.

Kayla ribbed him with her elbow and said, "Who do you think you are? Hugh Hefner? What's with the smooth talk?"

"Hey, now," he said, cocking his eyebrow. "I'm just being a good host, making sure my guests are comfortable and having a good time."

"It's really awesome, Jay," Rosemary said, grabbing Jason's hand that dangled from her shoulder. "And the guacamole is even better than usual, if that's possible."

"It's the secret ingredient that makes it so great," he said, looking from Rosemary to Kayla, both still under his arms. "Hey, Sara," he said, our eyes locking for the first time as Kayla and Rosemary discreetly unhooked themselves from his arms. Kirstie lingered for a moment, then headed off with the girls.

"Hey," I said, retucking my hair behind my ear.

"I'm glad you came. I wasn't sure if you would."

I wanted to say, *Are you crazy? I've been thinking about this every moment since you brought it up*, but that would have been totally lame, and besides, I think I was physically incapable of speaking. Instead, I stood there smiling, convinced I looked insane but unable to stop myself.

"You look really good," Jason said. "I like your shirt."

I rubbed my hand across my belly. "Thanks," I managed.

"So . . . ," he said, stepping closer to me, a little awkward on his walking cast, then leaned back against the table. "You like the guac? I made it myself. It's the one thing I know how to make."

"I love guacamole," I blurted. And then, I guess to prove to him that I meant it, I scooped some on a chip and popped it in my mouth. But I did it too fast, and a stray crumb went soaring to the back of my throat, starting me in on a coughing fit. My eyes stung with tears as I hacked uncontrollably. I could feel the tiny crumb lodged in the cave of my throat, but it seemed that no matter how hard I coughed, it refused to budge.

"Are you okay?" Jason asked as he patted my back. I searched for a drink—Kirstie never did bring me that Diet Coke. "Want me to get you some water?"

"Yes, please," I croaked.

"Be right back," he said, and he went off as fast as his leg would let him.

I desperately gulped for air as I kept on coughing. I tried to swallow, but nothing helped. I could feel the veins in my neck bulge, and people were starting to look at me.

"Ballbuster!"

I turned to see Shiner, grinning like he'd just made honor roll.

I spat out a couple more coughs while looking at Shiner. My abs hurt from the effort, and I wondered if I might pass out.

"Hey," he said. "You okay? Need a drink?" He held out the plastic cup he was holding. I looked at it suspiciously. "It's okay, I ain't got cooties," he said, reading my thoughts. I took the cup and gulped down bubbly Coke. I drank it so fast, it stung my eyes, but it seemed to do the trick—the crumb finally gave up and moved down my throat, a reminder tickle staying behind.

"Thanks," I finally managed, handing him back the empty cup. "What are you doing here?"

"Shoot, Busty. Same thing you're doing," he said. "Except I ain't hacking up chips like a cat with hairballs." For once he wasn't wearing his puffy Dallas Cowboys jacket, but he was wearing his coral necklace with a button-down shirt. He had even tucked in his shirt. Also, he smelled of Drakkar Noir—like, a lot of Drakkar Noir.

"What are you doing here? Were you invited?"

Shiner looked offended and said, "By the host himself. What are *you* doing here?"

"I was invited too." I hadn't meant my question to sound mean. "You guys friends now or something?"

"I mean, we're not best friends or nothing," he said, sounding a little insulted. "But, you know, since basketball we've been talking more at school about next season. Jason thinks I could make first string next year. Maybe it's just basketball, but I guess I finally found something I'm good at." He shrugged and said, matter-of-factly, "It makes people like me."

"Why do you care if these people like you?"

Shiner's skin didn't look great, but he looked like he'd gotten an actual haircut, not the choppy job he usually had. And he had made an effort to dress nice, even if his button-down was from Dollar General. It had to be—it looked exactly like the shirts my dad wore on the road.

"Thurman," he began. "There's something you ain't figured out yet."

"Haven't," I corrected, although I don't know why.

"You still *ain't* figured something out yet. Don't you know that you and me are a lot alike?" He took a step closer and moved his head to mine, conspiratorially. "I mean, come on. You're not going to stand there and tell me that you don't like Miss Rosemary Vickers talking to you? When people started to notice me on the basketball court, I felt like I got some respect, finally. It's nice when people take you seriously instead of seeing you as someone stupid. Right, ballbuster?" He smiled good-naturedly—his teeth were the color of chewed-up Double-mint gum, but his smile was goofy and truly happy. Looking at him, I couldn't believe that he and I wanted the same thing: to be seen as true contenders.

"I guess you're right." He smiled at me, proud but not arrogant. "Hey, I never did thank you for trying to warn me about the Mrs. Everly outfit. You didn't have to do that. And for helping me out with stats when I first started. That was really cool of you, so . . . thanks."

"What are you, on step nine or something?" My stomach dropped. How could he possibly know about the list? *But, wait,* I thought. There was no number nine on my Class Favorite list. Shiner said, "Ask for forgiveness? The twelve steps? Forget it. I was joking. I don't know why you're bringing all this up now, but okay. Apologies accepted."

"Hey, Moonshiner!" Jason approached us with a red plastic cup and handed it to me. "You feeling better?"

I nodded, and when he nudged my shoulder with his, I smiled as wide as I could without showing my teeth.

"So how's it going, man?" Jason asked Shiner. "You talked to Coach about next year?"

"Yeah," Shiner said. "He told me to talk to him on Monday. I guess we'll see."

"Hey," Jason asked, "is it true that it was your dad, Something Camry, who played in the eighty-nine game?"

"Yeah," he mumbled.

"That's pretty cool. You're, like, part of Bowie's legacy."

A hint of a smile formed on Shiner's mouth. "I guess I never thought of it like that."

"Hey," Jason said, turning to me. "Want me to show you around?" I vaguely remember nodding. "Cool. I'll see you in a while," Jason said to Shiner. We walked toward the entry hall where the stairs were, his hand resting lightly on my back—it sent tingles up my spine.

"Have fun," Shiner said as we walked away, and I swore I saw him wink.

What's Your Kissing Quotient?

When it comes to being kissed, you:

a) are just getting started.

b) have never been kissed.

c) could write the book.

"You want to see the coolest room in the house?"

Jason led me upstairs, taking them slow on his cast, and down a hardwood-floored hallway covered with a long, skinny rug. My palms sweated with the anticipation of what was about to happen. Quick flashes of us kissing darted through my brain. The walls were covered in faded photos of his family, dating all the way back from when Jason was in a crib—there was one of him holding a plastic rattle, and one with him and his sister, who was still in elementary school, hugging maniacally.

At the end of the hall, Jason turned a dull brass handle on

a door on the left. We stepped inside what looked like a small guest bedroom, with a white wicker double bed with matching nightstand, and lavender walls. My heart started racing, and I thought I might pass out from my sudden lack of breathing.

"You're going to love this," he whispered, a mischievous grin on his face.

This was the coolest room in the house? What guy would think wicker and lavender were cool? It looked like something my grandparents would love. "Yeah," I said, confused but trying to sound earnest. "It's nice."

I followed him into the room, anyway, and watched anxiously as he closed the door behind me with a soft *click*. I could hear the party going on downstairs, the laughing and the music, someone playfully yelling, "You cheated!" and I wondered, briefly, who had cheated at what.

Jason nodded toward the closet door. We crossed the room, and he opened the door deliberately, as if afraid of getting caught. I peeked over his shoulder with anticipation and saw clean white shelves stacked with dozens of board games: Trivial Pursuit, Outburst, Life, Monopoly—all the usual stuff. I wondered what he was looking for. The closet was a) not very romantic, and b) pretty small, with hardly enough room for the two of us to squeeze into. I didn't have a problem with being pressed up against Jason Andersen in tight quarters, but I wondered what the point was when we had this whole bed-and-breakfast–type room to ourselves?

"Uh . . . Jason?"

"Shhh . . . ," he whispered. "Follow me, but be quiet." He grabbed the center shelf, tossed one final wicked smile over his shoulder at me, and pulled the entire rack of shelves open like a door—a secret door.

He stepped through the back of the closet into a big, deep room with high ceilings. Jason turned back and took my hand, pulling me through the secret passageway. I stepped into the cavernous room, my eyes wide with excitement, overwhelmed by the beauty of the colors.

"Isn't it great?"

Kites hung above us—at least twenty of them, so many that I couldn't see the ceiling. Kites flew over kites, wide-winged ones up the highest, boxy and odd-shaped ones suspended underneath, tails hanging limp, waiting for a breeze to lift them skyward. The were all brightly colored, wings spread as if ready to take flight just as soon as that window in the back opened up. They weren't like kites I'd ever seen before—there was even one in the shape of a pig. The lights from the backyard shined up through the window, casting a candlelike glow into the room and through the kites. It was pretty awesome.

"Wow," was all I could gasp, realizing I'd been holding my breath as I took it all in.

"I love it in here," Jason said, looking around. "Well, I love it better when I get to take these out and fly them, but when I can't, I like to sit up here and just hang out, you know?"

I ripped my attention from the kites and noticed pamphlets and magazines scattered on the floor near a blue beanbag chair. One cover read *Kiting Journal of the American Kite Association*. "So . . . " I paused. "You like to fly kites?" Actually, the whole thing made me smile. I mean, kite flying? This meant that a bit of his inner geek from school years past hadn't totally escaped him. I liked that.

As if reading my mind, Jason replied, "Okay, so it's not like playing football or having paintball wars, but there's something about it. My dad bought me my first kite when I was seven or so and we were on vacation at Galveston. The kite wasn't anything special, but man, flying it was so cool. I kept letting the string out farther and farther, and it kept getting higher and higher until it was like a little orange and yellow dot in the sky." He looked at me, his eyes all shiny, even in the dark room. "I guess it sounds pretty stupid, huh?"

"No, no. Not at all." I searched for the right words. "Actually, I think it's really cool. I just didn't know, is all."

"It's not something I advertise. But I love it. My dad is helping me get into stunt kiting, where your kite does all these flips and twists. It's really hard to steer them, and you never know which way the wind is going to blow. The only thing between you and this big cool flying thing is a thin little string wrapped around a spindle." He paused, a little embarrassed, I guess, at going off again. "Anyway, I like it. I mean, yeah, I'm usually the youngest one at the kite events by about forty years, but the old-timers are cool. Not as grumpy as I would have thought. Just real nice."

"Wow," I said again. "That's really awesome, Jason." I couldn't help but think of the similarities between a stunt kite and my own life in the past few weeks, both up in the air, whipping wildly around in the wind, attached to Earth by one little fragile string. Instead of standing on solid ground, attempting to control my life, I had been the kite itself, up in the air, flapping and spazzing out. Like the kite, I had been at the mercy of the forces of nature and whoever and whatever held the handle down on the ground. I wanted to be like Jason, in control, trying to maneuver a kite through jaunty stunts, or maybe just to sail smoothly on the wind. It seemed like the harder I tried to gain control of my life in the last few weeks, the higher and farther I flew from the point of control. But then I realized that, lately, I *had* gotten more control of my life. I was finally realizing that I had the power to make things the way I wanted them to be. It was a pretty awesome feeling.

"Maybe someday you can come with me," he said. I gasped on the inside and tried to remain calm—couple-dom wouldn't be far away. "My dad and I are members of the Red Rivers

High Fliers, and we meet once a month at the VFW post. The old vets would sure get excited about a pretty girl coming to visit their club." He nudged my foot with his, and I smiled. It wasn't a dream ask-out, but it was pretty close. I liked the sound of the possibilities in our future together.

"Look," he said. "This might sound kind of lame, but don't tell anyone about this room. Or the kites. I don't really care if people know about it, but I kind of like keeping it to myself. It's something I only do with my dad."

I immediately knew exactly how he felt. It was like when I went with my dad to the shooting range. Even though I'm not exactly down with firing lethal weapons, it was always pretty awesome to have something that only Dad and I did. Like eating dinner at Luby's.

"I won't tell," I told him. "Not a soul."

He nudged me with his shoulder. "Come here," he said, walking to the window. "We can spy on them for once."

I looked down and saw several adults sitting in the backyard drinking wine. I recognized his mom, sitting with her legs crossed. She threw her head back and laughed easily.

We stared out the window for what seemed like ages, neither of us speaking. Jason took a deep breath and stuffed his hands in his pockets.

I played with my earlobe while I tried to think of something to say, but all I could think about was how I was standing in a secret room in Jason Andersen's house, that we were alone, and that once we finished doing whatever it was we were about to do, an amazing party still awaited us downstairs. I mean, how perfect was this night?

"You about ready for finals?" he asked.

"Not in the least. I've always been a bad test-taker."

"Oh, come on. What about that last algebra exam you killed on?"

"Please. That was pure luck."

"Hey, what about the brilliant tutoring?" He did that cocky-wicked-adorable smile that made my heart go *hum-an-a-hum-an-a*.

"Actually, I didn't learn a thing," I said, trying to keep calm. "Used a cheat sheet."

"Aw," he said, and grabbed my waist like he had on our library sorta-date, giving me a tickle that made me squeal like a total girly-girl. I tried to break free—from the tickling, not his hands—but he stopped, and leaned beside the window again. I looked out the window, wondering how I got to be here, in Jason Andersen's secret room.

"Whatcha thinking about?" he asked.

Instead of confessing any of the number of thoughts running through my mind—*do I smell, what is Arlene doing, will he kiss me, does this mean we're together?*—I asked him the question I really wanted to know the answer to, even if I looked dumb asking it. "How come?"

"How come what?"

"How come you asked me here tonight?"

Jason laughed, looking toward the window as he brushed his hair off his forehead. He looked back at me. "Are you serious?"

"I don't know," I said, realizing I was totally putting him on the spot *and* asking a stupid question. But I wanted to know. I folded my arms across my chest as a gesture of defiance. "Yes."

He laughed at my seriousness. "Okay, I'm game. Let's see . . . why do I like Sara Thurman. Hmm . . . let me count the ways. . . ."

"Forget it! That's not what I meant. I'm not fishing for compliments or anything."

"Then what do you mean?"

"I don't know." I suddenly felt stupid. To ask a guy why he likes you seemed like a good way to make him not like you. But I didn't get a lot of what was happening in my life right then, so I figured I might as well try to get one thing straight. Besides, why *would* Jason Andersen like me? I wasn't exactly a smooth kind of girl.

"It's just that," I continued, "I've known you since elementary school. And we've had English together this whole year. How come you just now started to like me?"

Jason sighed and said, "Well. I don't know. I guess I didn't really notice you before. I don't want this to sound harsh, but you've made it pretty hard to miss anything you do this year—or at least this semester."

"So you like a girl who loves making a fool of herself?" I was trying to sound hurt, but the truth is, I knew what he meant, and I liked that he was so honest.

"Maybe," he said. "But for a girl who gets herself in more . . . *situations* than anyone I've ever met, you're pretty good at staying cool through it all. Most girls would have started home-schooling the second they read the card on the flowers. And those things on your locker. . . ."

"Oh, God, please, Jason!" I buried my face in my hands in mortified embarrassment. "Don't ever talk about that again!"

He laughed. "You know what I mean. I guess I admire how, no matter what you're dealt with, you seem to take it all in stride. Most girls in our grade would have freaked out long ago. You just seem above all that." He *admired* me?! I couldn't believe that.

He looked at my lips, his eyes all soft, and before I knew it, he was leaning into my lips and we were kissing. I tried not to exhale too much, worried that my breath might stink of guacamole. I was also thinking, *Jason Andersen is kissing me. Oh, my god, Jason Andersen is kissing me!*

I tried to enjoy the moment, but I couldn't help thinking about how I should react once we stopped: Should I do a no-teeth-showing smile with flirty eyes? Or say something hot like, "That all you got?" Should I be aggressive and dive back in for more? Should I thank him?

It wasn't until we stopped that I realized how awesome kissing was. I'd heard slobbering stories about unfortunate first kisses, but with Jason, in the secret room at his party, kissing was sublime. And you can believe me, because I'd never use a word like *sublime* unless I really meant it.

Jason took a slight step back and, looking down at the carpet, asked, "You want to go back downstairs?"

I thought, *Um . . . no!!* But I nodded yes, and we started toward the door.

As Jason pushed open the door-shelf, he asked, "Hey, did you ever find out who did that to your locker?"

I thought of Arlene and how amazing she was for babysitting so I could be here with Jason, just like I'd been dreaming of. I thought of Kirstie, too, and how nice she'd been to me since first starting school here, but also how she hadn't made many other friends. I couldn't help but remember what Arlene had said about her: Just why was she so nice to me, so quickly?

"Never found out for sure," I told Jason. "But I know who didn't do it."

Do You Fight Fair?

Your sister has just accused you of stealing her favorite green cardigan ... again. You:

a) tell her she can shove her cardigan where the sun don't shine, then take her silver hoop earrings just to show her.

b) simply tell her you didn't take it, and refuse to continue the conversation if she persists.

c) tell on her for falsely accusing you, and try to get her grounded for it.

As Jason and I left the secret room and walked down the stairs, I felt like we were royalty, walking regally, with our people below us. I saw Olivia Randall, whose locker was in the same hallway as mine, do a double-take when she saw us, and Richie Adams did the same. I thought I heard the quiet gasps of Bowie students, and then the frantic whispering of the new gossip: Him? With *her*? I'm not sure people actually said that, but it wouldn't have surprised me. I still couldn't believe it myself. *Me?* With *him?* But there I was, and there we were. And it felt pretty great and surprisingly comfortable.

Everyone was crowded in the living room, and the music was louder than I remembered. It looked like everyone was having a great time, and with Jason there with me, it was turning out to be a stellar night—one of the best ever.

Shiner sat on the edge of the beige couch, people-watching as he drank from his plastic cup. He looked at me sort of knowingly—it was something in the way he held his mouth, slightly nodding his head. Like he approved, but not in a gross way.

"Jason!" Rosemary called as she and Kayla scooted over to the three of us by the couch, all smiles. "So, uh . . . where've y'all been, huh?"

I was busted and loved it—I felt a sense of pride, like now everyone knew we had sneaked off to a private room upstairs. A smile forced its way onto my embarrassed face, but I was shocked when I glanced at Jason and *he* was blushing. Rosemary said, "Yeah. That's what we thought," and I was so completely flustered, except this time it wasn't the mortifying kind I was used to.

Looking at Jason, his cheeks flushed red, and at Shiner and Rosemary and even Kayla, all of us hanging out, I just couldn't help laughing—it was so crazy! Had my CF list really worked, or was it my own self that got me there? Did these people really like me, or did they just like me because Jason did? It didn't matter: I was at a party with the unapproachables, and now they seemed like regular people—except maybe better-looking. The only thing that was missing was Arlene, I sadly realized.

Kirstie approached us and nudged herself between me and Rosemary, who stood near me but not right next to me. I refrained from dragging her by the wrist off to a corner to divulge all the kissing details. In a lowered voice, she said, "You abandoned me. Thanks a lot."

She seemed upset, but Rosemary joked, "She abandoned all of us."

"Hey, where's your friend I used to always see you hanging out with?" Kayla asked me. "Marlene?"

"Arlene," I corrected, a sudden pang shooting through my stomach. I didn't want anything bad happening tonight, but she had been in the back of my mind all evening.

"Right," Rosemary said. "I thought y'all were inseparable or something."

"We got in a fight," I said. I could feel Kirstie's eyes on me, and I knew she felt for me.

"Really?" Rosemary asked. "What happened?"

Nervousness began to build inside me, and everyone's eyes

were on me, waiting for a response while Kirstie fiddled with the edges of her hair. I didn't want everyone to know our business, so I just said, "Oh, nothing. We'll be fine."

Kayla said, "Hey, I've been wondering. Did you ever find out who trashed your locker?"

I did not want to talk about that or remember it, especially when the night was going so well. I shook my head. "No, but it doesn't matter. It's over with."

"Can you imagine what it takes for a person to do that to someone?" Rosemary asked.

"Totally," Kayla agreed.

"But I'm glad you're okay now," Rosemary said. "At least, you seem to be."

"With Sara, you can never be sure," Jason teased as he put his hand on my lower back. "She's probably hyperventilating on the inside." I smiled and nudged him.

It felt amazing to have their support, but I couldn't help but notice a weird vibe zooming around our circle. Kirstie kept a vigilant watch on the carpet, while Shiner's eyes darted from Kirstie to me to the floor.

A moment that seemed like eternity passed as we all looked around at one another. Finally, Shiner spoke up.

"If you don't tell her, I will." Shiner looked at Kirstie, who stood as still as a wax figure.

"What?" she managed.

"You better tell her," he pressed.

"What's going on?" I asked, looking between them. Shiner shook his head, like he was disappointed. I looked to Kirstie. "What is it?"

She looked like she was going to cry. Kirstie Luegner, who I always thought could take on anyone in any room, was on the verge of tears. And for what?

Kirstie mumbled, "The thing about your locker . . ." She looked up at me, but quickly dropped her eyes down again. "Look, the thing is, it's . . . I know who did it."

Everyone was staring at Kirstie, eagerly awaiting what she had to say. I had a feeling what was coming, but whatever she told me, I decided it was between the two of us. There was no reason for everyone to hear. Plus, without all the prying eyes, she might be more honest—with herself and with me.

"Come here," I said, pulling her into the entry hall for privacy. I could feel her hand shaking. "What's going on?"

She took a deep breath. "I have to tell you something." I nodded. "I've sort of been lying to you."

"Sort of?"

"Okay. Massively. Remember how I told you I was voted Most Popular at my old school? Well, I wasn't. I've never been popular. I just said that so you'd think I was cool or something." I waited for her to say more. "The truth is, I don't know how to make friends. You'd think I would, after all the moving we've done, but I don't. I just fake it, or pretend to be important until someone—anyone—lets me in. Pretty pathetic, huh?"

"I don't know," I said, because I honestly didn't. I didn't know what it was like to move around a lot, but I did know that when Arlene and I stopped talking, I was clueless as to how to make new friends. "You didn't have to lie, though. You're a really nice person."

"Yeah, well, tell it to the people at my last school," she said. "What I did there was awful. You think you get embarrassed. . . ."

"I doubt you have anything that can top my embarrassments."

"Your embarrassments—they were all out of your control. The only thing that was in your control was how you handled everything, and you handled it all brilliantly. Not like me." She shook her head, her eyes welling up. "At my last school, I was just so tired of moving and trying to start over. I got too desperate, too fast for friends. There was this one girl—you could take one look at her and know she was popular. We were both in the bathroom between classes one day, and I offered her twenty bucks to be my friend. I don't know what I was thinking. As soon as I said it, I regretted it. But then she started laughing. She was all, 'What did you say?' Real loud. Soon everyone heard about it. It was awful. I had no one until I moved here." She wiped away a tear that ran down her cheek.

"When I saw you in the office—and heard why you got those flowers—I thought you were someone that I could, not just be friends with, but someone I could take care of. You don't know what it's like, always being alone. I don't have any brothers or sisters, and my mom's been taking care of us both since I was born. No one's ever needed me. I just wanted to matter."

"Wait, you heard who sent me those flowers while you were in the office? You knew about them before I did—before Arlene did." I couldn't believe it. "It was you who spread the word about them, wasn't it?"

Kirstie couldn't even look me in the eyes. I barely heard her peep, "Yes."

"God, I can't believe it," I said, because it was a lot to take in. "You did *everything*. I can't . . . and you did that thing to my locker, what—so I'd rush to you? So you could rescue me or something?"

She shrugged. "Sort of. I knew that Arlene didn't like me off the bat, and if I just got her out of the picture, then we could be friends. And we were. Weren't we?" she asked hopefully.

"Kirstie, this is really messed up," I said. "I can't believe you'd do something like that to someone you supposedly care about. It's so wrong."

"I know! And I'm so sorry! I'm such a jerk. I don't expect you to forgive me, but I hope you can. You're a really sweet girl, Sara. Way better than some Haden Prescott phony." She smiled.

I shook my head. Suddenly the whole Class Favorite thing seemed so silly and trite. What had I been doing, making lists and trying to get friends who had never given me the time of day before? I'd had a great friend in Arlene who'd always been there for me, and I'd dumped her for Kirstie, the sole person who was responsible for my unhappiness the past couple of months. And Kirstie did it all on purpose, for selfish reasons. "I don't know, Kirstie. I need some time to process this."

She nodded.

"You're joking, right? Because this is the most uncool thing I've ever heard." We turned to see Kayla and Rosemary standing in the doorway by the living room. It was Rosemary who had spoken, which surprised me. Rosemary had never gotten mad in front of anyone before, and she'd certainly never spoken to someone so harshly before. The party turned its attention to our group, everyone staring. I could hear the whispers and see the eyes locked on Kirstie, and even in my anger and confusion, I felt a little sorry for her. I knew how she felt right then, being in the center of a screwup. Except she had done it to herself, which, actually, probably felt worse.

"Y'all, it's okay," I said to the girls, who looked like they were ready for blood. Kayla, I could see, was getting a bit aggressive. But Rosemary? I didn't know it was in her.

"Dang, girl," Kayla said to Kirstie. "That's low."

"Real low," Rosemary said, her arms folded across her chest.

"I'm a jerk, okay?" Kirstie said, her voice cracking. "I'm a stupid little jerk. And I didn't mean for the locker thing to be so bad, but once I got started, I just couldn't stop. Ever since that day, and especially since you blew up The Ball"—she looked to me—"I've felt extra awful."

"Is that why you gave me this shirt? And brought me that other one back from Aspen? Didn't you learn your lesson the first time?"

"I know! I said I feel horrible."

"Feeling and doing are two different things," Kayla said. "And you even ratted her out about the flowers? Sara was your only friend when no one else was."

"Exactly," Rosemary said.

"Y'all, seriously, wait," I said. It seemed like everyone was watching us, and I hated that. I didn't want anyone to go through the humiliation I'd endured during the locker incident—even the person who did it to me. "Leave her alone. She's apologized. Now it's between us."

"You sure?" Jason asked. He looked at me like he was concerned for me, not like he wanted me to give Kirstie hell.

I nodded and said, "I'm sure."

And then, he surprised me. He looked to Kirstie and asked her, "You okay?"

She blinked and said, "Yeah. Yes, I'm fine. Thanks." Tears began to roll down her face, which she quickly brushed away.

"Whenever I feel down," Jason said seriously, "all I have to do is think of the stampede that started with the sound of The Ball exploding." He winked at me. "Always puts a smile to my face."

I knew he was just trying to smooth things over, and it did help a bit, but I still couldn't believe that it had been Kirstie who had done those horrible things to me in the past couple of months. All the doubts Arlene had had about her were right.

The attention seemed to move away from us, and I saw more tears roll down Kirstie's cheeks. She called Jason's name and motioned him toward her. I couldn't hear them, but he took her into the room just off the entry hall. When he came out, he let out a deep sigh.

"She's calling her mom." I nodded. "I think she wants to stay in there until her ride gets here."

"That's fine," I said. "I can't really handle talking to her now. You know?"

"I know," he said. "You're a really good friend, Sara. You didn't deserve all that stuff that happened to you."

"Thanks," I said.

We hung out in the living room with the others as the party wound down. I should have been happy—Jason, his party, the support of Rosemary and Kayla that made me feel like an accepted member of their group. But I wasn't happy, and it wasn't just because of Kirstie. I had been betrayed, but in many ways I felt that I had let myself be betrayed. Not believing Arlene had been my biggest mistake, and nothing would be right until I tried to fix that.

The only problem was, I had a feeling it was too late for us.

♥22♥

Do you have a forgiving nature?

You let your friend borrow your brand-new, very favorite white skirt. She returns it with a huge spaghetti stain on it that no amount of dry cleaning can remove. She apologizes again and again, and you:

a) tell her it's okay, but vow never to let her borrow anything of yours ever again.

b) tell her you can never trust her again—she knew how much that skirt meant to you.

c) tell her you know it was an accident, and forgive her completely.

"Hey, Thurman. You okay?" Shiner was sitting outside on the bottom porch step. He had offered me a ride home just as I was about to call my mom, and I accepted. Jason had hugged me good night, asked again if I was okay, and promised to call me.

"Yeah, I'm okay."

"My brother's on his way. He should be here any second."

"Cool," I said, sitting beside him on the step. I thought of the day I had sat with him out in the field after I found my locker. I realized more and more what it meant to have the support of real friends—including Shiner. I was glad we'd moved on from the mean comments, or from pointedly ignoring each other. "Hey, how did you know it was Kirstie?"

"You know the day it happened, the same day I got kicked out of Ms. Weaver's class? I roamed the halls for a while, deciding if I was actually going to go to Principal Moran's office. I saw Kirstie in the halls, carrying a box and a bunch of wrappers to the bathroom. They were in a plastic bag, but I could see through it. To be honest, I wasn't a hundred percent sure until she started confessing everything."

"I still can't believe it," I said.

"Listen, Thurman," Shiner began, keeping his eyes down on the ground. "I was thinking. It was so stupid what happened between us last year at that dumb dance. I'm sorry for all the rude things I've said to you since then." He glanced at me and said, "Even the ones you don't know about."

"I probably deserved some of them," I confessed. Shiner had proven himself to be a totally awesome human being. When Arlene hadn't been there—or rather, when I had banished her from my life—it had been Shiner who was there for me, helping me pick myself up when I got knocked down, like when I blew up The Ball, or even right then—taking me home when I felt I'd been totally crushed by Kirstie's admission of guilt.

"You're all right, Thurman. You know that?"

"Yep. I know. Hey," I said. "Do you think your brother could take me somewhere instead of home? It's still on the way."

He shrugged. "Sure. He's got nothing better to do."

His brother pulled up in his dull, beat-up El Camino, complete with FEAR THIS emblazoned across the back window.

I sat squeezed between Shiner and his brother, Jackson. We were all quiet during the short drive; the only talking we did was my giving Jackson directions. I thought about the events of the night, and wondered what life would be like on Monday.

When Jackson parked his car in front of the Medinas' house, Shiner opened the door and we both got out.

"Want us to wait? How're you going to get home?"

Looking at the house, I said, "Either I'll get a ride with Arlene, or I'll be calling my mom in about two minutes." I tried to smile, but inside, I was nervous about seeing Arlene. "Don't worry about it. I'll be fine. And thanks, Shiner. For everything."

A smile lingered on his thin lips. "Anytime," he said.

Arlene stood hiding behind the Medinas' front door like she was afraid I might attack at any moment, but when she spoke, her voice was kind, if questioning. "What are you doing here?"

"I, uh . . . ," I began. I realized I didn't know what to say. Well, I knew what to say—*I'm sorry for being such an jerk!*—but I didn't know how to say it with the deep, heartfelt gratitude I felt for her.

She looked over my shoulder. "Who's that lurking out there?"

I turned to see the El Camino still idling at the curb. "Oh, that's Shiner. He and his brother gave me a ride." It wasn't until I waved at them that the car clicked into gear and slowly drove away.

"Shiner?" Arlene said, eyeing me curiously. "Must have been some party."

"You don't know the half of it. The *fourth* of it," I said. "Is it okay if I come in?"

Arlene toed the edge of the door with her foot. "I guess. But be quiet. The twins are asleep."

Inside, Arlene plopped down on the plaid couch and folded her legs up under her. On the television, a blurry image of Mariah Carey either singing or yelling was frozen on the screen. I knew instantly it was *Glitter*, a Golden Raspberry we had both wanted to see. When Arlene saw me looking at the screen, she snatched the remote and clicked the TV off. She sighed heavily, and I knew she was gearing up to really give it to me. I sat in Mr. Medina's Barcalounger and waited.

"We were supposed to be best friends," she began, her voice tight. "You've ruined everything. Why did you have to be such brat, huh?" Her voice was rising, but she didn't seem to care. "I tried to tell you before, but you didn't seem to care about the truth, but I'll tell you again: *I didn't know about those stupid flowers your mom sent.* And I wasn't the one who plastered your locker. And tonight sucked, for your information, so I hope your party was worth it." She lowered her voice and said through gritted teeth, "I don't even know why I did this for you. I guess I'm just so stupid that I don't even know how not to be your friend." Tears welled up in Arlene's eyes, and it was the first time I'd seen her cry since her grandma died years ago.

"Arlene, I'm so sorry," I pleaded. "You have no idea what's been going on."

"You were awful to me," she cried, her eyes begging for understanding. "I didn't realize until you weren't around how much I talk to you and how much we're always together. When you stopped talking to me, I felt like . . . I don't know . . ." Her eyes looked up at the ceiling, searching for the right words. ". . . a losing Lotto ticket—worthless and tossed away." She sniffled, looking down at her hands in her lap. "I felt like the biggest loser," she cried.

I couldn't stand it anymore. I rushed over to the couch and sat down beside her. "Please, *please* don't cry," I begged, my eyes stinging with tears and my nose becoming snotty. "I'm awful, and you're *not* a loser. The thing is, I know how you felt. But at least you had Ellen and your other softball friends. I've felt totally left out of your life since you started playing softball. And then I just got jealous, I guess. I was jealous that you had made so many new friends and I didn't. I guess that's one of the reasons why I was so quick to be friends with Kirstie. I wanted to show you that I didn't need you." She looked hurt when I said that. "But then I realized that I do need you. You're my best friend."

Arlene wiped tears from her cheeks. "I didn't mean to make you feel left out. We still did the movie thing."

"I know," I said. "But that's not the same thing as hanging out every weekend. Look, I'm so *so* sorry about everything that's happened. I swear on everything that is good and holy that I will never treat you like that again. You're the only friend I ever want to have. Can we please be friends again?"

Arlene wiped her nose on the back of her hand, then wiped her hand on her jeans. A smile emerged on her tear-stained face, and for the first time since I'd told her my parents were getting a divorce, Arlene and I hugged. As we squeezed each other tight, she whispered, "*Best* friends."

♥23♥

Will They Remember You
When You're Gone?

What yearbook award best describes you?

a) Most Popular—everyone knew me, I knew everyone, but my circle of friends was tight (i.e., elite).

b) Most Congenial—everyone knew me, I knew everyone, and we all loved one another.

c) Newcomer Award—even though you've been at this school for four years.

After all that, I wasn't only nominated—I won.

This is what it had all come down to—this day. Being in that room full of winners, and actually being one of them, felt a little surreal. I simply couldn't believe I was there. I'd always wondered what it was like, all those accomplished people gathered together for the yearbook photos a couple of weeks before the end of school, and now I knew. For all of Bowie eternity, I would be seen as one of *those* people. And I really liked that—I deserved to be proud of myself.

There were no cheese-and-cracker platters like I had imagined, no Cokes or bottled water on any tables, but the scene was still amazing. Everyone was crammed into the library, where we were photographed against the same blue backdrop they'd used for our class pictures. While I waited for my turn, I found myself hovering somewhere between the winners of the Most Versatile Award and the John Philip Sousa Award for music, feeling awkward and nervous about having to smile in front of all these people. I was waiting for them to turn to me and yell, "Just joking!" and laugh me out of the school.

"Hey, Thurman."

Shiner stood beside me, wearing a blue blazer that was a little short in the sleeves, with a striped tie that hung too low over his belt. He stood really straight with his shoulders all squared and a pretty satisfied grin on his face.

"You look nice," I said, looking down at his duds, and I meant it. I eyed his jeans and ratty sneakers with the blazer and tie.

He shrugged. "Only the waist up, right?"

"Good point. I got this," I said, and I pulled on the new necklace I got from my dad when he returned from New Mexico. It was a tiny turquoise butterfly on a silver chain, and

I loved it. Finally, I thought, something that lets me know that he doesn't think I'm a kid anymore.

"That's nice," Shiner said of my necklace.

When Mrs. Waxman called Shiner, he stepped up to the stage with Ellen Spitz for the One to Watch Awards.

"Scoot closer, Jimmy!" Mrs. Waxman commanded. "She's not going to bite you!"

Ellen blushed as bright as her ruffled blouse—she was Westernless, for once—and somebody called out, "She might, if you ask her nice!"

I felt so proud to see Shiner standing up there, finally being recognized. He deserved it more than anyone.

"They'd make a cute couple, wouldn't they?"

I turned to see Jason standing beside me. He looked almost like a grown man in his dark blue suit and bright red tie. He even had polished dress shoes on. He put his hands in his pockets and rocked back on his heels. My dad used to do that.

Jason and I hadn't exactly become Bowie's new power couple like I had hoped. We talked a lot at school, walked the halls together a couple of times a day, and he sometimes stopped by my locker in the mornings. My heart raced every time I heard his voice on the phone, which I did, several times a week. Everything was great . . . except we hadn't actually gone out yet. I really liked him and wondered if I should ask him out, but I wasn't surprised that the year was ending and we weren't an official couple. It had all been a fantasy, anyway.

"So, well, congratulations," he said.

"Yeah, thanks. You too."

We silently watched as the seventh-grade Class Favorites took their places in front of the camera, the guy resting his hands on the girl's waist.

Even though I still felt butterflies around him, I'd long since decided to stop trying too hard and to just *be.* "Tell me, Andersen. You're totally jealous of my award, aren't you? Come on, you can admit it."

"You're crazy," Jason said, smiling. "It's cool you're here, Sara. And not just because of the award."

I smiled and tucked my hair behind my ear.

"Let's go!" Mrs. Waxman called. "Eighth-grade Class Favorites, step on up!"

"Smile pretty," I said as Jason turned to take the mini-stage. I stood content as Jason and Rosemary Vickers had their Class Favorite pictures taken, just like they deserved.

I shouldn't have been surprised when the yearbooks came out and I saw my picture. My left eye was half-closed, and it barely looked like I was smiling.

"I told that photographer guy I wasn't ready yet," I said to Arlene, Ellen, and Kirstie, cringing at my image forever emblazoned in Bowie's pages.

"It's still pretty cool," Ellen said.

Beneath my picture read:

> **"Courage is grace under pressure."**
> **—*Ernest Hemingway (1899–1961)***
> **Courage Award**
> **Sara Thurman**

I was really proud of my award. Like most things that had happened this semester, I totally didn't see it coming. When I didn't get nominated for Class Favorite, I realized I wasn't the least bit bummed. The whole thing had been superficial and immature. The Courage Award, on the other hand, made me realize that people saw something in me that I didn't see in myself. Somehow, I had become—or maybe had always been—someone who took things in stride. That's a good thing, because life moves and changes pretty fast sometimes, and even though I can't control that, I know I can control how I react to it.

As for Kirstie—yeah, I did forgive her. And even though what she did to me was horrible, and she should have been the one to come to me, I decided to go to her. After all the avoiding I had done with Arlene, I decided that, if I thought the friendship was worth it, I should make the first move. And I believed Kirstie was worth it.

"I just want you to know," I told her before science class the week after Jason's party, "that I get why you did it. You did a horrible thing—the meanest thing anyone has ever done to me—but I understand."

Kirstie looked beaten and tired. Her black hair was dull, and her green eyes didn't seem so bright. "What do you mean? What I did was inexcusable—"

"It was," I insisted. "But I understand the desperation you felt. It's like how desperate I was to make people like me. Or did you forget about the list of Class Favorite qualities I used to carry around with me?"

She smiled. "I didn't forget. Look, I'm not proud of what I did."

"I'm not proud of what I did either. But I know you're sorry, and I want you to know that you have a real friend in me. You don't have to force our friendship. It was always there."

Kind of like my courage, I had thought, hidden beneath all my insecurities.

As Arlene, Ellen, Kirstie, and I stood huddled around our yearbooks, someone called out my name. We all turned in unison to see Jason approaching us.

"Hey," I said, a smile spreading across my face.

"Look," Jason began, his eyes glued to the floor. "I was wondering . . ."

Thankfully, Arlene, Ellen, and Kirstie stepped off to the side, but they didn't go far. I knew they were straining to hear every word.

"I was wondering," he said again. "I've got a kite competition coming up. It's this Saturday afternoon, and I thought we could go get a pizza or something after. It's not a big deal—I probably won't even place." He hooked his backpack up on his shoulder, looking nervously around him. "Anyway, I was just wondering if you wanted to go? With me. If you want. I mean, it'll be no big deal."

I looked at Arlene, who was eyeing me. This Saturday was our Razzie night, and Jason just had to pick this weekend to finally ask me out. Just my luck.

"That sounds awesome," I said, "but the thing is . . ." I had this knotted mess in the pit of my stomach, even though I knew what I wanted to say. "Well, the thing is, I kinda already have plans." I spoke quickly to keep him planted beside me. "Is there another competition coming up? Or maybe we could just go one afternoon. I could do it if it were any other Saturday. Really. I mean it, Jason."

He looked back at me, and I smiled.

"I'll hold you to it," he said. "The old-timers at the VFW are dying to meet you."

"Dying—don't say that!" I said. But what I was really thinking was, *He's been talking about me!*

Jason laughed and said, "You're so crazy," which made me beam.

After he walked away, Arlene punched me in the arm and shrieked, "Are you crazy?! What were you thinking? Why would you turn him down?"

"Because," I said, enjoying the sight of her mouth gaping open, and still a little shaky myself, "the only place I want to be Saturday night is with all my friends, watching one Razzie movie and one Oscar winner. It's gonna be great."

As we pushed through the front doors of the school, my stomach finally settled down. I thought of Jason and the date I knew we'd have and of Saturday night with Arlene, finally having our cherished little ritual again with the added bonus of having new recruits Ellen and Kirstie. I also knew that, for me, there was lots more to come. All I had to do was relax and act normal.

Like myself.

Which Yearbook Award Will YOU Receive?
Take This Quiz to Find Out!

Chapter 1
Does Your Crush Know You Exist?

You're walking—okay, drooling—along behind your crush when he unknowingly drops a pen from his backpack. You hurry to pick it up; when you give it to him, he says:

    a) nothing, just accepts the pen and keeps walking.

    b) "Thanks," and smiles at you before moving on.

    c) "Thanks. How'd you do on that geometry quiz last week?"

Chapter 2
Are You the Keeper of Secrets or the Disher of Gossip?

You've stepped out of your sociology class to go to the bathroom. On the way back, you hear Angie Slater whispering into her cell phone, saying, "I can't believe Joann got suspended for plagiarism." You:

    a) discreetly walk away, but decide to tell *only* your best friend, and *only* after making her swear not to tell another single living soul.

    b) tell no one, since the news doesn't even affect you.

    c) shuffle away quickly, heart racing with excitement. When you get back to class, you tell what's-her-name across the aisle what you just heard.

Chapter 3

Can You Turn Your Sibling Spats into Something Special?

True or False: When it comes to sharing clothes, your sister knows that what's yours is hers, and vice versa.

Chapter 4

Are You Open to New Friendships?

A new girl arrives in your civics class and asks you if she can sit with you at lunch. You:

    a) ask her what type of clique she hung out in at her last school so you can fairly decide if she's a fit for your clique.

    b) tell her of course she can sit with you, and you'll meet her at her locker and escort her to the cafeteria just to make sure she doesn't get lost.

    c) tell her, *"No habla English."* Why is that stranger talking to you?!

Chapter 5

Do You Stand Out from the Crowd, or Blend In with the Scenery?

At the spring dance, you decide to be bold and try out some new dance moves. What happens?

    a) A circle forms around you, some people laughing, some cheering you on, but soon, everyone is mimicking your stellar moves.

b) A few people around you ask if you're having an epileptic fit.

c) The dance goes on just the same.

Chapter 6
Do You Know Who You Can Trust?

You really need to talk to your best friend about the latest development in the on-going saga of your love life, but she's not at school today. Instead, there's Veronica, a relatively new girl you've become friendly with. What do you do?

a) Tell her your problem, automatically assuming that she'll keep the information mum.

b) Tell her your problem, but make her swear on her cat's life that she won't tell a soul.

c) Wait and call your best friend when you get home—you'd rather not take the risk.

Chapter 7
Do You Have What It Takes to Be the Coolest Kid in Class?

Which word best describes your attitude toward popularity?

a) superficial

b) (my) reality

c) unachievable

Chapter 8

Can You Exude Beauty in an Ugly Situation?

You're strutting through the food court wearing your killer new cream-colored pants, when a five-year-old menace comes racing through the aisles, smearing your pants with ketchup and mustard. How do you react?

- a) By screaming at the kid for ruining your clothes and telling his mother she's an unfit parent
- b) By "accidentally" tripping the kid on the way back to his table
- c) By laughing it off, saying that your dull pants now look like a Jackson Pollock painting

Chapter 9

Are You Overly Emotional?

The guy you've been crushing on just said your new haircut is "really interesting." How do you react?

- a) By faking cramps and going home to cry in bed for the next two days. You knew you looked like a freak!
- b) You tell him, "Thank you," and agree that the new style is interesting and unique.
- c) By demanding to know exactly what he means by "interesting"? Is he insulting you?!

Chapter 10
Are Your Parents Totally Unfair or
Are You Totally Unreasonable?

Just as you're heading out the door to meet Mara and Eileen at the movies, your mother stops you and says you have to do the dishes before you leave. How do you react?

a) By refusing to do them until you get home—even if it means groundation

b) By asking your mother if you could please do them as soon as you get home

c) By doing them right away, even though that means missing the previews—your favorite part of any movie

Chapter 11
Find Your Inner Flirt

You're finally ready to—subtly—let Lucas know you think he's totally hot. While you're both in the lunch line, you:

a) wink at him, smile, and walk away.

b) briefly make eye contact before grabbing a Snapple and bolting to your table.

c) get behind him in line, tell him you like his jeans, and ask him, with a hint of coy, why the two of you haven't hooked up yet.

Chapter 12

What Your Spring Style Says About You

On the first warm day of spring, you're most likely to be seen wearing:

a) the same black clothes you wore during winter, except maybe your shirt is short sleeved instead of long sleeved

b) jeans, sneakers, and a comfortable tee—something that will allow you to pop into an impromptu soccer game if need be

c) the most adorable spaghetti-strapped sundress, even though it's still a little chilly out

Chapter 13

Can You Tell a Friend from a Foe?

You lost a note from your friend, Casey, which had some very private information on it regarding her—*gulp!*—"female freshness" problem. To make matters worse, most of the football team found out. She said she forgives you; now, you need to confide in her about the problems your parents are having. Is there a chance she'll turn on you, just to get even?

a) Slight chance—I'd be leery of telling her anything too big, too soon.

b) No chance, no way, no how.

c) Big chance—I can't ever tell her another secret as long as I live.

Chapter 14

Does He Like You . . . Like That?

Testing the waters, you tell your friend and heart's desire, Stefan, that the new guy in history is totally cute. He:

a) scoffs and says, "You can do better!"

b) nods and says, "Yeah, he's like the female version of that smokin' Brazilian babe in our homeroom."

c) doesn't even look up, just mumbles, "Whatever."

Chapter 15

What's Your Rep?

You just won an award for Most Conscientious Recycler in your town. How does your school respond?

a) By surprising you with a full-page ad in the local paper congratulating you

b) Only your two closest friends know, because they're the only ones you told.

c) Your school doesn't respond, but at least your parents are proud of you.

Chapter 16

Be Honest:

Do You Love, Like, or Hate Gossip?

You have just been told that your economics teacher, Mr. Russo, has been performing in a play downtown. What do you do?

    a) You e-mail the entire school directory with the news, including the when/where/cost of the play, and try to rally everyone to go see him—it'll be a huge laugh!

    b) Tell your closest friends, giggle about it, but wonder if it's true.

    c) Shrug off the information—there's nothing to back up its truth, and besides, even if it *is* true, he's still an awesome teacher.

Chapter 17

Are You a Stand-up Stephanie or a Push-Over Penelope?

You have a huge term paper due tomorrow. Your best friend, Alexis, calls and begs you to go with her to the mall, where she knows her ex-boyfriend will be hanging out with his new girl. After she swears she'll never ask for another favor again, you:

    a) agree only after she starts crying and asking how you can be so mean to someone you call "friend."

    b) agree only if she buys you dinner at Wok 'N Roll.

c) tell her that you love her, but you have much more important things to do—and so should she.

Chapter 18
Are You Really Best Friends Forever?
True or False: I know that I can trust my best friend with anything I tell her.

Chapter 19
Do You Know How to Party?
Your swim team just had its third victory in a row, so you invite the team over on Saturday night to celebrate. The vibe is:

a) raucous—come as you are, bring who you please, and turn the noise up!

b) low-key—only the girls on the team are invited for a movie-watching marathon complete with tons of junk food.

c) elegant—below-the-knee skirts are a must at the three-course dinner you're catering.

Chapter 20
What's Your Kissing Quotient?
When it comes to being kissed, you:

a) are just getting started.

b) have never been kissed.

c) could write the book.

Chapter 21
Do You Fight Fair?

Your sister has just accused you of stealing her favorite green cardigan . . . again. You:

a) tell her she can shove her cardigan where the sun don't shine, then take her silver hoop earrings just to show her.

b) simply tell her you didn't take it, and refuse to continue the conversation if she persists.

c) tell on her for falsely accusing you, and try to get her grounded for it.

Chapter 22
Do You Have a Forgiving Nature?

You let your friend borrow your brand-new, very favorite white skirt. She returns it with a huge spaghetti stain on it that no amount of dry cleaning can remove. She apologizes again and again, and you:

a) tell her it's okay, but vow never to let her borrow anything of yours ever again.

b) tell her you can never trust her again—she knew how much that skirt meant to you.

c) tell her you know it was an accident, and forgive her
completely.

Chapter 23
Will They Remember You When You're Gone?

What yearbook award best describes you?

a) Most Popular—everyone knew me, I knew everyone,
but my circle of friends was tight (i.e., elite).

b) Most Congenial—everyone knew me, I knew everyone, and we all loved one another.

c) Newcomer Award—even though you've been at this
school for four years.

Chapter 1
A = 1
B = 2
C = 3

Chapter 2
A = 1
B = 2
C = 3

Chapter 3
T = 2
F = 1

Chapter 4
A = 3
B = 2
C = 1

Chapter 5
A = 3
B = 2
C = 1

Chapter 6
A = 2
B = 3
C = 1

Chapter 7
A = 2
B = 3
C = 1

Chapter 8
A = 3
B = 1
C = 2

Chapter 9
A = 3
B = 2
C = 1

Chapter 10
A = 3
B = 1
C = 2

Chapter 11
A = 2
B = 1
C = 3

Chapter 12
A = 1
B = 2
C = 3

Chapter 13
A = 2
B = 1
C = 3

Chapter 14
A = 3
B = 2
C = 1

Chapter 15
A = 3
B = 2
C = 1

Chapter 16
A = 3
B = 2
C = 1

Chapter 17
A = 1
B = 3
C = 2

Chapter 18
T = 3
F = 1

Chapter 19
A = 3
B = 2
C = 1

Chapter 20
A = 2
B = 1
C = 3

Chapter 21
A = 3
B = 2
C = 1

Chapter 22
A = 1
B = 3
C = 2

Chapter 23
A = 3
B = 2
C = 1

Which Yearbook Award Will You Receive?

Scoring Results:

51–65

Most Outspoken

You're full of life and energy and make it a habit to stand up for yourself. But be careful: *Outspoken* can sometimes be another word for *stubborn*. You're headstrong and not afraid to flirt or let your opinions be known, and that's a good thing—until you're offensive or say something inappropriate. Soften up a bit and remember: It's not always all about you. Give others the spotlight sometimes. A little humility goes a long way.

33–50

Sweetest Girl

You're the girl everyone wants to be friends with and every guy wants to take to the dance. You care about your friends, but you don't believe in exclusivity and you almost always give people the benefit of the doubt. You make the best of difficult situations. You're confident, upfront, and honest—without being a turn off.

22–32

Most Likely to Be Left Behind on a Field Trip

Being low-key is one thing, but being downright invisible is another! Learn to take chances instead of always doing what you know to be safe. You're a good, loyal friend, but don't let people take advantage of you. Trust your instincts and question things that don't feel right. There's a fierce extrovert somewhere inside you—let her out every now and then!

Taylor Morris is a native Texan who wrote her first novel in the fourth grade. It was twelve pages long and called *Love at First Sight*. Her first published book was called *Original Divas: All-True Tales from the World's Most Fabulous Stage and Screen Divas*. When Taylor's not writing, she loves to hike, but she hates to run, and she plays dodgeball once a week. Taylor subscribes to many magazines, most of which are for girls much younger than she is, but she reads them all cover to cover. Some of her own stories have even appeared in these magazines, including *Girls Life*, which has published her short stories and articles. Taylor has lived in six cities in four states in nine years, and now happily resides in New York City with her orchestra conductor husband, Silas, and their two cats, who have a hyphenated last name. You can visit her at www.taylormorris.com.